TRUEBOY

TRUEBOY

THE STORY OF A GREAT DOG

By Thomas C. Hinkle

WILDSIDE PRESS

To

Author's Note

MANY of the incidents in this story are taken from life. Trueboy is based on a real character. He was a big, cross-bred dog owned by my grandfather, Casper Hinkle, who was a great hunter in the days when hunting meant danger. This splendid dog followed the danger trail from dawn until dark, asking nothing more than to be near his human friend. A mighty dog was Trueboy, yet when the hunter spoke to him he was all love and would come up to press his warm tongue against his master's cheek.

The incident of the dog and the little coyote is also based on fact. Years ago, in the hills of central Kansas, a big dog of mine became very playful and affectionate with a young wild coyote. Many times I saw them playing at a distance but when I tried to approach, the little coyote would be off as fast as he could go.

I grew up in the West with horses and dogs

as my constant companions, and I have never understood why some people put all dogs in one class. Dogs are as different one from another as are men. Some are naturally good, some are bad. What makes a good dog *stay* good, even though he suffers for it? I do not know; but I do know there have always been dogs who would not go back on their good instincts even to save their lives. I will never forget the big dog I once knew who, by a strange circumstance, was helpless and starving, and at the same time close by some little pigs. So badly did he need food that he could have eaten them all, yet he would not touch them. He knew what pigs were and that they were not for him. Loyal to the last, he would not break faith with man. Happily, the dog was found and lived.

If the story of Trueboy makes some reader a little more appreciative of what a good dog really can mean to a man the book will have been worth while.

T. C. H.

Ottawa, Kansas.

Contents

[ix]

TRUEBOY

Chapter I

IF the puppy, Trueboy, had been given his way that morning he would not have left his home in the haystack on a Far Western range. But a man being master of the little dog, he and his sister, Nannie, were picked up from their sleep very early in the morning, and dropped into their present uncomfortable quarters, a feed box at the rear of a lumber wagon.

All day they had been traveling, and it was late afternoon.

Very weary and painful was the ordeal for both pups but it was exceedingly so for Trueboy. The black-and-white female, much smaller than he, was able often to sleep on her side of the box, but only on occasions did Trueboy doze a little. This greatest adventure of his life kept him awake, alert, miserable.

Trueboy was a beautiful pup. He was jet black with four snow-white feet. His eyes were a luminous, yellowish hue, with something wistful, anxious in them. And even at this age, Trueboy pricked his ears up straight, as he looked over the box.

Nannie was again sleeping on her side of the box but he sat up looking out. This was so different to him from the days and nights when he was with Nannie and his mother in the haystack. He could play then, and as often as he wished, he could lie down in the nest and go to sleep. And when he awakened he could romp with Nannie until they were both tired, when they could peacefully go to sleep again. He was terribly sleepy now— sleepy and so weary, yet he could find no rest. He tried many times to lie down like Nannie, but always something awakened him with a start so he again sat up and looked out.

Trueboy could not understand it all. Where was his mother? Why did she not come near where he could see her? At times he stood up with a quick, searching look and

as often as he did this he uttered a little plead-
ing whine. Why did she not see him and
come near him? If *she* would only come,
things would be at once made right. They
always had. Once he could not stand it, and
he cried out loudly for her. But the creaking of the slow-moving thing that held him
was the only answer. After that Trueboy was
silent.

Sometimes he saw a crow fly near the wagon
and even in his unhappiness he looked with
interest and wondered what it was. He also
looked with curiosity on small herds of cattle
grazing on the valley and he was instinctively
afraid of them.

Once he made a desperate effort to get out
of the box but this was impossible and he did
not try again. He only sat now, and looked
and waited—for what, he did not know.

Old Bill Henley, the owner of this outfit,
sitting on the front seat, driving, had put the
pups in their uncomfortable quarters because
he had forgotten them until every place in the
wagon was filled with other things.

Henley cared for the pups as he would have cared for any friendless thing that had lately lost a mother; but they were, nevertheless, a burden to him. As he drove slowly along he wondered to whom he could give them. Henley was on a still hunt. He knew a reward of several thousand dollars was offered for a big cattle-killing gray wolf of the range. Bill wanted the reward and he had faith in himself. He supposed that by the time fall came, or at latest early winter, he would come in with the pelt of the Old Roarer to claim the reward. Henley wanted to roam over the range, camping wherever he chose, and hunt quietly in his own way. These two little pups made extra work for him.

Suddenly Old Bill stirred out of his doze. The wagon clattered down over the broad, flat stones at the foot of the hill. He pulled up quick and hard on his horses to allow the wagon to come slowly to the level ground; at the same time he saw a horseman galloping towards him across the valley. On came the rider with the ease of a flying bird, his horse kicking up little clouds of dust that floated in the rear.

"Dan Hudson!" exclaimed the old man to himself as he recognized the boy, who with his father owned the thousands of acres over which he was riding. The rider galloped up alongside and reined in his sweating mount.

Young Dan was eighteen, six feet tall, lithe and wiry in build. His keen gray eyes took in quickly every detail around him. Besides his lariat rope he carried a rifle which protruded from a leather holster on his saddle. Henley knew the rifle was always in readiness to bring down the big timber wolf, and the old man was a bit doubtful of his own prowess as he looked at the youth. Yet Dan had already tried for a year and had failed.

"Hello, Bill!" Dan greeted the old wanderer in a friendly manner. "Seen anything of the big wolf to-day?"

"Yes," Old Bill replied slowly, "I saw him this morning at the bottom of the Flint Hills, but he was a long ways off. I didn't shoot. He was 'way out of range and slipped down into a gully the minute he saw me. But he's likely twenty miles from there now, Dan; no use to try to get close 'nough to shoot him. I hear your father's raised the reward; how much is it?" he broke off suddenly.

"Four thousand dollars," said Dan, holding up his horse that was champing at the bit and dancing about impatiently. "He'll pay that much"—Dan added—"he decided a week ago." Dan wheeled his horse and was starting away when he saw the heads of the two lonesome pups in the feed box. He smiled eagerly, dismounted, and came up to look at them.

"What are you going to do with these pups, Bill?" he asked.

"Sure 'nough, I clean forgot," said Bill. "Give 'em to you, Dan, if you'll take 'em. They're mighty nice pups, and mighty smart ones too; they're going to make awful big dogs some day. Their mother was a big smooth-haired collie and their father was the biggest dog I ever saw. He weighed one hundred and eighty pounds; he was coal black and could fight like a tiger. Had some great Dane and Irish wolf hound in him. I wish I could have got him after the big wolf—but he and the collie both got poisoned."

Dan stood caressing the pups and Bill got out to stand beside him. "Dan, ain't that little black one a beauty! He's jet black with four white feet just like his father, but he's got the fine yellowish eyes of his mother. We named him Trueboy; the female's just plain Nannie. But I got no time to fool with pups."

Dan lifted Trueboy out of the box, sat down on the ground beside him, and said: "You bet I'll take him, Bill. I'll take the other one, too, if it will help you out. I'd take a dozen just to get *him*. Why, he's absolutely the prettiest pup I ever saw!"

Trueboy gamboled about a little, then suddenly stopped and turning his head to one side looked quizzically at Dan, then because he was glad, and afraid, he barked sharply. Dan laughed and shook him a little. Trueboy wanted to play but Dan was anxious to be off.

He put him back in the box, saying, "Will

you leave them at the ranch house, then, Bill?"

"Sure," replied the old man. "I'll leave 'em with your cook. I reckon Pete'll look after 'em."

"He will," said Dan. "Much obliged, Bill. Now you're sure you'll leave them both?"

"Of course, Dan. That's all I want—just to *give* 'em to you. They'll be there when you get back!"

With a final pat on the head of the little black pup, Dan rode away to forget about the pups for the exciting business of hunting for the cattle-killing wolf and the small band that followed him.

On riding around the spur of a hill he came suddenly in sight of a bunch of cattle, bawling and milling around some object at the edge of a swale below. Dan put his horse rapidly down the sloping ground toward the excited cattle. He soon saw the cause of the trouble. The carcass of a half-eaten heifer lay on a patch of wet sand near the water-filled swale.

Dan dismounted and, leading his horse, bent over to examine the ground carefully.

"Wolves!" he ejaculated. The footprints of the beasts were plainly visible in the moist sand. The track of the huge wolf showed here and there—a track that was twice the size of any of the others. Dan judged the kill was a recent one, perhaps done in the night just passed, or possibly in the morning of this day. There was no use in looking longer at the kill —the trail of the wolves was the thing. Dan followed the tracks some distance until he lost them in a stretch of rough ground; but when he saw that the trail led northward he mounted and rode in that direction. He kept his right hand free to lay hold of his rifle, while his eyes searched everywhere in the distance before him.

The huge gray wolf that Dan was trying to catch sight of on his swing up the valley was known far and wide among the cattlemen as Old Roarer. He got his name from his deep bass roar that easily distinguished him from others of his kind. For three years traps, guns and poison had been tried and for three years all had failed. Cattlemen with heavy bore rifles hunted him day after day and week after week, but the cunning Old Roarer spurned them all; he went on with his killing and his wild nightly roars were heard in any part of the range he chose to roam.

Three miles Dan rode down the valley. Nothing greeted his eyes but the herds of red, black, and spotted cattle feeding on the wide valley. He turned sharply to the west to look at some wolf traps set at the mouth of the Custer Gorge. The first four he examined were not sprung, yet wolves had been near them for he found their tracks. The fifth trap was sprung although by what means Dan could not tell, for there was no hair in the trap jaws.

On a stretch of level ground near some water holes a little farther on, Dan picked up the trail of the Old Roarer. By leading the horse and watching carefully he was able to follow the trail a long distance. The tracks were so fresh that Dan got his rifle in his hands to be ready at an instant's notice. On and on the keen-eyed boy plodded along the sands of winding draws; over dry run beds of finest loam, where tracking was easy; or near the muddy margins of scattering water holes, sometimes losing the trail altogether, at times picking it up again by a single track, and sometimes by nothing but a single scratch on the hard ground, until the footprints at last faded out among some scattering trees and bushes.

Dan gave it up, mounted his horse and rode away toward the ranch on the Big Pine River. As he cantered along his thoughts for some time were centered on the big wolf and how to find him, when suddenly the two little pups came to mind, and particularly the little black fellow that Dan had loved the instant he saw him.

As he rode along night fell; the stars peeped out; the moon pushed up above the hills in the east, and a cool night breeze fanned the boy's face. But Dan took no notice of the night and its coolness, in his thoughts of the little black pup.

[23]

An hour later he rode up to the ranch house. He put his horse away and went at once into the cook house to greet good-natured Pete.

"Pete, I'm as hungry as a bear, but let me see my pups first. Where are they?"

"Shucks, Dan," said Pete with a sympathetic look as he turned from his work at the stove, "it's too bad, I hate it too. Old Bill Henley drove up here late this evening and said he'd promised to bring you two awful good pups, but said he lost them out of the feed box behind his wagon on the way—said he went back a long ways and looked but couldn't find any sign of 'em—said he guessed you'd have to give 'em up for likely the wolves or some other varmint would have 'em before morning."

Dan stood still for a moment simply looking his disappointment; then without a word he washed his face in the tin basin on the bench, wiped slowly with the towel, hung it up on its accustomed nail and said:

"If I thought there was any use I'd go out and hunt for them to-night. I liked that little black pup in particular—looked like he might make a great wolf dog. But I'll wait and start early in the morning along the back trail of Old Bill; I may run across them yet."

Chapter II

WHEN the lumber wagon rattled on that afternoon, and Dan Hudson rode away from the two pups in the feed box, Trueboy climbed up to look after his receding form, and whimpered because he had to stay behind. He wanted to get out on the ground.

As the jolting wagon moved along, Trueboy tried to play with Nannie by reaching over the cross-piece in the box, and chewing her neck. Each time he tried it, however, the hind wheels of the wagon dropped into a rut or struck an unusually large stone, so that he gave up his play to look out behind and be miserable.

The plodding horses crossed the valley to a point where the trail led up a steep hill bordered on the left by a rocky gorge. At the bottom of the hill Old Bill stopped to let his horses breathe a little; then started on. From

[26]

the first it was bad going. The hind wheels of
the wagon struck the round rocks with such
force that the puppies were knocked about
until they whimpered with pain. Suddenly
there came a violent lurch of the wagon; one
hind wheel struck a big rock; the other
dropped hard into a deep rut on the edge next
to the gorge. The pups shot out of the box
into the air and turned over and over until
they struck the bottom of the gorge. Old Bill
was shouting, and lashing his horses franti-
cally to prevent the wagon from going over.
Almost by a miracle he saved himself; then
berated and scolded his horses until he was
over the hill and away from danger.

In his excitement the frustrated old man
forgot all about the pups. He drove on,
complaining to himself about the rough going.

Poor Trueboy and Nannie!

At the bottom of the gorge where the puppies fell was a swiftly moving stream bordered on either side by a low ledge of solid
rock. Nannie struck full on the ledge; after
a slight quiver her troubles were over. True-

boy missed death by two feet. He fell just over the ledge into the deep water. When he struck the stream he was dazed and blinded, but came up struggling. Gasping for breath, he struck out bravely, and the current carried him to the pebbly bank not far below. He stood for a time dripping and breathing hard. Then he slowly padded up along the pebbles to the broad, rocky ledge, searching for Nannie.

He found her lying very still on the rock. He nosed her and tried to awaken her, but she did not move and something told him there was no use. He looked anxiously at the little form lying there so quiet, then around him, and a great loneliness came over him. He wanted to get away but he did not know how or where. After hesitating a little he set out down the gorge. He went along slowly, nosing the thickets here and there, stopping often to look around, for everything in the gorge was strange and threatening, even the sounds of the stream lapping the edges of the rocks where he stood; the high trees and bushes, and great rocky wall of the gorge itself, alarmed him. He kept near the water and passed on until he came out where the gorge spread into a level fan; here he stood at a point in the forest where the stream broadened and flowed quietly along with a gentle murmuring sound.

The evening fell as he entered the woods and the darkness of night was settling down. Trueboy stopped and looked back, but he decided to go on into the forest because he feared the open spaces more than the shadows among the trees.

He wandered on until he came to a large thicket the outer branches of which curved over to the ground. Afraid and hungry, he crept under this shelter. For some time he lay trembling and shivering, but at last, so tired he could not hold his eyes open, he fell asleep.

Within an hour a chill wind sprang up. It blew into his shelter and awakened him with its cold touch, for he was still wet from his plunge in the stream. He raised his head and listened; no sound except the wind blowing through the tall pine trees reached his ears. A little later his eyes told him that enemies were not only near but, what made it worse, enemies that moved without making the slightest noise.

Three times he saw forms move past him down the stream, yet he heard not a sound. Suddenly came a rushing through some bushes above and a timber wolf ran by. Trueboy was so badly frightened he would have run away if there had been time, but the wolf ran out of sight as quickly as he came.

There was no sleep now. Trueboy lay still, with all his muscles tense. While he watched he held his ears erect. This was one of his striking characteristics, a thing that was born in him. His collie mother before him had held her ears erect, and so had his giant father.

He lay and watched in the stillness for several minutes after the wolf had passed. Then suddenly came a sound that sent terror

through him, although it was the first time
in his life he had heard it. A great horned
owl on silent wings swung low over the
thicket to sound his frightful "who-whoo-
whooo." Some inner voice told Trueboy that
this flying thing was as dangerous to him as
the menacing form of the running wolf or any
of these other enemies—they were all alike to
him. Frightened and miserable while the
shadow passed over him, he crouched down
in the thicket, without making a sound.

As the minutes passed, Trueboy's mind was
at times dimly on Old Bill, and sometimes he
thought of Nannie; fear all but crowded out
his thoughts of her, yet more than anything
else he wished he were back in the haystack,
cuddled up against Nannie, and free from all
this miserable uncertainty.

For a time there was stillness, but the stillness itself, and the strangeness, troubled him.
He noticed the slightest rustle of a leaf or vine
over him; the faintest snap of a twig; even the
low whispers of the wind through the pines
spoke danger to his ears.

The hours passed.

Never relaxing, he lay where, in the gray of the morning, a flock of teal ducks whistled over the thicket and frightened him again, but he settled down when he saw them alight on the water and swim quacking down the stream.

When the sun was an hour high he came timidly out.

The same friendly instinct that had told him to hide in the thicket now told him it was time to leave his cover for water and food.

He stood outside, afraid to advance, but he was very thirsty and the running water was before him, and he could not resist. He must take his chances. A new light had come into his eyes during the night. It was the wild, watchful light of all wild things. This light shone in his eyes while he stood on the edge of the stream, lapping the water, but continually raising his head to watch for enemies. He had nearly finished his drinking when there came thumping sounds on a rise of ground above him in the thickets and trees.

With his nerves on edge Trueboy did not wait to see what it was; he ran for the thicket and darted under.

Fainter and fainter grew the sounds, and he was quite content to lie still until they died away altogether.

This was bad luck for Trueboy; the instinct that before had been his best friend here played him a cruel trick. For he stayed hidden in the thicket while Dan Hudson hunted for him everywhere except in the place where he lay.

Chapter III

DANGER EVERYWHERE

CAUTIOUSLY Trueboy started through the woods. Never in his short life had he been so hungry. Yet he saw not a single thing to eat. In the days when he lived with Bill Henley the old man set bread and milk before him in generous quantities. Now it was far different. It was at that time in the spring when bugs and other insects were just beginning to stir in the warming rays of sunlight. As to rabbits, squirrels and other small game Trueboy could not have caught them had he tried; and, at this stage of his life, he would not have tried even though one of them had stopped directly in front of him.

He walked slowly through the woods to a long open space by the margin of the stream where two aged, dying cedars with barren, straggling limbs, a thin covering of foliage on their top, stood close together, leaning over the water. Near the cedars lay an old log, decayed from the rains of many summers. In a hollow at one end of this log Trueboy came upon a number of black bugs. They darted about in lively fashion, but he caught nearly all of them. Immediately he began to hunt along the log for more. He walked the entire length of it on the side nearest the stream; moved around and passed along the opposite side to the other end when he quickly dropped flat on the ground—only his nose and eyes beyond the log.

A stoat, hot on the trail of a rabbit, was coming on, following the edge of the stream. It ran past with sinister, arched body, its small murderous eyes telling of its deadly intent. Trueboy, with frightened eyes, watched until it disappeared in a brush tangle up the creek. When he raised his head to look there were no more enemies in sight; it looked safe enough to move down the stream again.

From the two old cedars, around a bend in the water, there stretched a long level covered only with tall, withered grass and low, greening bushes. Trueboy moved on, keeping well to this cover, until he passed the entire length of the open and emerged into the woods below.

All was still around him, but he was very suspicious. He started on among the trees and had covered several rods when the sudden, harsh cry of a bluejay overhead made him dodge as if he had been struck. And again, near the water, the angry bark of a red squirrel frightened him. He wandered timidly and watchfully along, not knowing what he might come to, and fearing the worst at every step, when his course led him to a clearing at the edge of the forest, where for many miles one could see out on the open range. He sat down and looked across the valley, undecided what to do. The walking was easy in the open beyond him; there were no trees nor bushes in the way, yet the open alarmed him. Every place for that matter was strange and forbidding, but there was something about the long level valley beyond that told him he should not go far out in that direction.

DANGER EVERYWHERE

To the left of the valley the ground rose and fell in gentle swells until it reached some distant foothills, beyond which towered the giant peaks of the snow-capped mountains. Trueboy sat at the larger end of a grassy arm that reached far down into the near-by forest. He covered the grassy space at a run. Not far in these woods he came upon a great mass of decayed wood. No bugs were in sight but his keen nose told him to search for them, which he immediately did by pawing away portions of the soft decayed wood. Under an unusually large mass he found many grubs, every one of which he licked up quickly, but they only whetted his appetite.

Picking his way carefully around great clumps of underbrush and prickly overhanging vines, dense growths of sprouts, and tangles of brier-covered thickets, he reached a point where the timber changed noticeably. There was now and then a willow tree growing near the edge of the water, and here and there a great cottonwood with its thousands of beautiful, rich green leaves murmuring in the soft wind. But the changing woods meant nothing to Trueboy. He went on in that same distress of mind as when he started. / If he should continue in his present course he would finally enter the woods along the ever-restless, tossing waters of the Big Pine River. For a long distance down the Little Pine he held his course, at times seeing only frisking chipmunks near their holes in stumps, or red squirrels scolding angrily at him from the tall trees, and often the screaming bluejays whom he already disliked with something akin to anger, because they frightened him.

As he traveled the woods became heavier. He found himself among dense thickets and underbrush, and for a tedious hour he threaded his way in many time-losing detours, trying to get into the open. Sometimes when he passed near the water's edge, he came upon a great willow or cottonwood leaning far out over the stream. Sometimes he stopped, afraid to pass great masses of vines that burdened the tall branches of thickets; once he stopped at a bend in the stream where the current, partly blocked in its course by a drift-heap, rushed and swirled angrily around the great tangle of logs and sticks. The deep, rushing water frightened him. He backed away from the edge of the bank and trotted into the woods farther away from the stream.

In this timid, cautious fashion little True-boy hunted all forenoon. Once he came upon a wood mouse and leaped for it, but he was so clumsy it escaped him. In a small clearing near some tall shrubs he stopped before another log, and remembering the bugs and grubs he had already found in such places, he immediately began to scratch the rotten wood. While he worked away he heard a slight sound behind him; he looked up just in time to see a black bear walk around a thicket and out near the log. It was a mutual surprise. The bear instantly rushed at him and Trueboy, yelping and terror-stricken, ran dodging and shooting around thickets like a rabbit—never stopping to look back until he found himself again near the bank of the creek. He peered out from the underbrush and discovered that the big black bear was standing at the log, tearing away the dead wood with his terrible paws and feasting on the insects and grubs that Trueboy had wanted.

With his hair standing erect on his neck and shoulders, his ears laid back on his head, Trueboy ran down near the margin of the creek.

He was so badly frightened by this black monster that when he came to a dense vine-covered thicket, half a mile away, he crept into its shadows and watched for an hour before venturing forth again.

The big enemy was so hideous that Trueboy could not forget. He understood that one of these huge black creatures might be met with in any direction.

After a long time, the profound stillness in the forest having reassured him, he came forth to start again through the woods, but looked back often to see if the black monster was pursuing him. While he hurried on he was so frightened he forgot his hunger; he

forgot his thirst; he forgot that it was growing dark.

Night fell, and it fell suddenly in the heavy
forest. As it happened he stood near the flow-
ing water, and breathing in the fresh damp
coolness from the stream reminded him that
he was starving for a drink. He had poked
only his head through some thin bushes at the
top of a gentle slope that led down to a long,
level, sandy shore. The space below, which
was suddenly lighted when the moon pushed
up over the trees, was open except for a clump
of bushes situated about midway below on the
level sandy shore. Trueboy pushed through
the bushes above and stood looking. One
night in the woods had been enough to make
the intelligent little dog know that there had
suddenly come into his life danger, danger
everywhere—and thirsty as he was if he
quenched his thirst at all, he must stand in
danger while he drank.

Chapter IV

THE moon pushed up over the trees and lighted the sandy open shore below like shadowy day. The longer Trueboy stood and watched for enemies the more he looked at the vine-covered thicket standing alone down on the wide sandy level. Every shelter lured the pup; the thicket with its dense tangle of vines lured him now. A little wind blew across the water and directly into his face as he looked down on the bright moonlit space. Moving slowly, looking on both sides of him and twice turning to look behind, he walked down to the water's edge with the lone thicket a little to his right. He reasoned that the dense thicket would hide him from any prowling enemies above in the woods. Seeing no movement about him, he lapped the water eagerly, straining his eyes to look while he drank.

A FEARFUL NIGHT

Suddenly, and without the least warning, for there was no sound, a shadow swooped down upon him and a great horned owl seized him with its claws. Trueboy had whirled like a flash and saved the middle of his body but the claws sank in just above his tail. With a cry of mortal terror he rushed for the near-by thicket. The owl tried to hold him, the while beating him with its powerful wings, but Trueboy made the thicket and pulled in as far as he could with the pain of half a dozen knives cutting him. The owl, seeing his prey partly escaping, strove desperately to pull him forth by flapping its wings while snapping at him with his beak and hissing like a snake.

After the first agonizing cry Trueboy turned and fought desperately, showing in this, his first deadly encounter, the kind of stuff he was made of. The pain in his tender flesh was maddening but he uttered only low whines and deadly snarls while he struggled and fought. His efforts broke the hold of one of the owl's feet; Trueboy turned around and snapped savagely. He chopped into the elbow of a wing; he did not let go but held, jerked back and ground his dagger-like teeth into the bone, doing terrible execution. With the vines in its way, the owl, suddenly put on the defensive, flopped its other wing, snapped viciously with its beak to free itself, but Trueboy only jerked the harder, ground in his teeth and shook the thing like a rat. One tremendous tug backward and he tore away the portion of the wing and fell back into the thicket, free. With one wing broken, the big owl backed away, walked about on the open sand cracking his beak, hissing, and futilely flapping the one wing in an effort to fly.

Trueboy lay in the center of the thicket, spitting feathers from his mouth and uttering short whimpers of pain. Caution, however, quickly got the better of him; he lay still, alternately licking his wounds and looking out at the hissing, flopping owl. Then Trueboy forgot his wounds; he forgot everything but the shadowy form of another creature. It moved down on the sand, making no sound.

Slowly, steadily, it approached. Something told Trueboy that the animal, a big lynx, was coming for the owl. He watched intently as the wild thing came on. Twice it stopped and crouched flat to the sand, crept forward quickly and crouched again. The big owl was walking about, cracking his beak and hissing as if to drive his enemies away by the very fierceness of his actions. The bird gave no sign that it saw the enemy until there was a sudden rush, and the gray body of the lynx shot out in the moonlight.

The big cat seized his victim. There came his low growls mingled with the hissing of the owl as the bird sank the claws of one foot in the gray hide. There followed a great scattering of feathers and then all was still except for the low, angry growls of the lynx. He ate mincingly of his kill, but it offered little to his taste. There were more feathers than meat and the meat itself was extremely tough and tasteless—good enough for a lynx starving in winter, but not good enough now when there were other and plumper wild things to be had.

Growling still, and licking his fangs, the lynx padded softly down the creek and vanished in the shadows of the trees.

With every muscle tense Trueboy watched. The little wind blew steadily across the stream into his thicket. In his inexperience he did not know that this steady breeze was a very friendly one to him—a wind that carried his scent away from wild animals passing between him and the creek. On the other hand, should a hunting wild animal circle the sand above the thicket, the wind would be deadly dangerous. But again in his inexperience Trueboy did not know this. Time after time he wanted to run away, but being afraid to run, he only lay still.

Again, from the dark shadows up the stream on the moonlit sand, he saw the form of some animal coming down. On it came, the stealthy, quick-moving form of a mink. It stopped suddenly on seeing the form of the owl, looked sharply all around as if suspicious that the killer of the victim might be near, then ran up to the carcass, tore at the feed and snarled as it ate. While the mink fed, its odor was blown to the moist nose of Trueboy, an odor much stronger than that of the lynx or owl. But the creature left quickly for he, too, was looking for something juicier than owl. He ran over the sand near the water and vanished in the shadows like the lynx.

This was Trueboy's second night in the wild, and a fearful night it was. He was learning, but learning against his will. Trueboy did not know he was lying near a wild animal trail. He knew only that he was lying where there were many enemies, and his only chance was to hide and keep still.

As time passed the wind stiffened. Once a dead twig fell on his shelter and frightened him to a standing position; he lay down again only to get up immediately. He saw out of the corner of his eye a slight movement to the left, and soon the gray form of a big coyote emerged, making little more sound than the lynx. He trotted up to the remains of the owl, and shook and scattered it in every direction. He did this as if he were going to be good enough to tell the next hunter that there was nothing here worth having. Having finished his play, he stood still, listening. A cottontail ran past; the coyote shot after it and vanished like a puff of smoke.

Again all was still.

For some time nothing but the wind moaning through the trees, or the far distant "whowhoo" of an owl reached Trueboy's ears. He again felt his wounds and he had just begun to try to ease them by licking them gently when he pricked up his ears again in fright.

Two bobcats, headed toward the owl, entered the bright sandy shore from opposite directions. They saw one another at the same instant, and from their actions, they were evidently old enemies. At any rate they were well matched as to temper. They moved slowly toward each other, stepping stiffly and growling low. When the space of a few feet separated them they were all over each other in a flash. It was a fast and furious battle with teeth and claws and whirling, tumbling cats emitting shrieks of rage that reverberated far up and down the forest. It ended suddenly—as quickly as it began, and the bobcats ran in opposite directions. Probably they both decided at the same time that they had had enough of that business.

Trueboy lay in a miserable tension while the night dragged slowly to the dawn.

When broad daylight came, he crept, stiff and sore, out of his shelter. He looked timidly at the remains of the owl, but there was too much danger here to feed. He circled to the trees above and again wandered down the woods not far from the stream. In his own uncertain way Trueboy was trying to find the kind of surroundings that he had so much loved and had lost, and lost in a way he never could understand.

Far down in the forest he came to a place on the edge of the woods where the ground fell gradually away to a level, rocky barren around a willow-bordered swale below. The swale ended, some distance away, in an abrupt, high rocky hill. Trueboy sat down to ponder the situation. Which way should he go now?

At first the wrong voice spoke. It told him to go down the long incline and into the woods along the swale. He started, but got no more than ten feet when he stopped. In some bushes to his right he saw a black bear moving and instantly another directly behind the first. Only their heads and backs showed above the bushes, but that was enough. Trueboy had had enough of bears. He turned back into the woods and ran swiftly until he came once more near the Little Pine Creek. Then he settled down into a trot which he held steadily for several miles. Tired, hungry and thirsty, he came out of the woods near the stream to a place that attracted him at once. The lonely little puppy had not found what he wanted more than anything else in the world, a human friend. Nevertheless, this place seemed to invite him for it apparently offered some shelter from the great strain that was always upon him, and so he decided to stay for a while.

Chapter V

THE HOMELESS PUPPY

THE spot lured Trueboy for several reasons. It proved at once to be a better place for feeding and hiding than any he had seen since his battle with the owl. The stream widened here, and there was a broad level stretch of sand on this side, bordered above by a heavy growth of timber. Just beyond Trueboy, where he stood looking down the stream, was a high irregular wall of rocky cliffs back some yards from the stream; broken here and there with steep sloping earthy banks on which scrubby bushes grew. At the base of these banks were many crevices and small holes making excellent hiding places for small animals.

As Trueboy started for the nearest hole he came upon a great find—a freshly killed rabbit only half eaten. He fell to the feed and for the first time in many hours satisfied his appetite. He walked out over the sand to the edge of the creek, and after a long satisfying drink came back to the hole. It was at the base of the steep, rocky bank and looked like a good hiding place.

He did not go in at once, but stood for a minute looking up and down the stream; across into the woods on the other side, and into the trees behind him above the sandy shore. Nothing moved but a bird here and there, and no suspicious sound reached his ears. He turned and sniffed in the hole. There was no warning scent; he went in. It was only a short pocket a few feet back in the rock, but there was dirt enough on the bottom to make a comfortable bed; it gave him a sure protection from every side except the front approach. He stretched out comfortably and slept for several hours.

Trueboy's first days in this place were pleasant enough, or as pleasant as they might be without another puppy or a human companion for him to play with. Trueboy was one of those dogs in which the desire for play was strongly implanted—a dog that would still enjoy a romp with a pup at four or five years of age. But he made his own fun here by running out on the sand, biting bits of wood, tossing them and chasing them; then lying and watching them out of the corner of his eye in make-believe fashion, as if he did not see them. Sometimes he would seize a shell and toss it, sending it spinning on the sand and then would race after it, capture it and hold it between his paws, all the while trying to make himself believe it was a real live thing trying to get away from him. Some days he ate well, but on others he got so hungry he had no play left in him.

One day while wandering along the level sandy shore he came upon a small shallow pool only an inch or two deep where some minnows had been left by the rapidly falling water. He succeeded in getting them all; this was the second good meal since he had been lost. At the end of ten days, Trueboy had grown thin and he was always hungry. By making many short excursions into the woods above, he managed to get enough bugs and other insects to keep him alive, but that was all. After his hunger got so persistent, he spent very little time in his hole, and even the darkness found him hunting.

One night he pounced upon a wood-rat and had quite a tussle. It bit him savagely, but he finished it quickly. The strain of this constant warfare was telling on him. It was not only the difficulty he had in getting food for himself, but there was the constant danger of being devoured by some enemy. Necessity, however, did one good thing for him; it made even his caution more intelligent. When he heard the loud "who-whoo" of an owl he understood the sound, and quickly got under cover to look above him and listen. At these times he was in no hurry to come out, but waited until he felt safe again.

Early one night he made his way among the trees and underbrush, hunting for the least morsel of food. It was a night of heavy black clouds; moaning wind and threatening rumbles of thunder—a night when miserable

Trueboy would have stayed in if he could, but he was slowly starving. An hour of worried hunting brought him nothing; and he might have hunted all night if Nature had not compelled him to do otherwise. The thunder rumbled louder and almost continually; the rain began pelting down, at first in big scattering drops, then before Trueboy could make any distance the water was driving down in sheets through the open spaces of the forest. Trueboy was so badly frightened he thought only of one thing—his hole in the rock. Blindly he headed for it but every time he came to a rift in the trees he was struck by a blinding torrent of rain. And what was worse, he found that dangerous wild things were running for shelter like himself.

He rushed under the low-hanging branches of a pine, plump into a weasel that had run in from the opposite side. The weasel had no more than struck than it sank its fangs into him. It had no time to select its point, but got its teeth into Trueboy's flank. Trueboy uttered one sharp cry of fright and pain, then swept his head around and sank his own teeth into the middle of the weasel. He ground his teeth in and shook and shook and shook until he held only the limp body.

He was so hungry he fell to the feed at once and had half finished when the wet form of a bobcat swept under the tree. Trueboy's quick eyes and legs saved him. He shot out while the bobcat contented itself with the remains of the weasel.

Badly buffeted by the driving storm, Trueboy ran on, made the creek bank and stumbled over to a point above his hole. He struggled back in the teeth of the storm and, drenched and shivering, got in. But his troubles were far from over. He panted and licked himself for some time when he started up with the feel of cold water around him. There came peal after peal of crashing thunder; lightning lit up the flood like lurid day. Trueboy whimpered anxiously. The angry water surged past, getting rapidly higher, and telling him plainly enough that it would soon be over him.

THE HOMELESS PUPPY

With a shiver and a gasp he plunged into the flood. The swirling waters at first covered him completely. The current, where he plunged in, swung in like a thing alive and swept him out into the torrent. But again, far down, after it had half drowned him, it whirled him in like a bit of bark; he felt the ground beneath his feet, struggled up the bank, and dropped down exhausted. The rain beat upon him. He got to his feet, struggled to a thicket and crept in. It was poor shelter but he was afraid to seek a better one.

The fury of the storm finally spent itself, the rain fell in a gentle shower and at last there were no sounds but the dripping of the water from the rain-drenched trees. All night Trueboy lay shivering, with his golden-brown eyes peering into the darkness.

When morning came he moved out into the open. It was a cool, dripping woods that greeted him; a sweet fragrance was in the air; a freshness about every thicket, log and leafy bush. But Trueboy noticed none of it. The loneliness that had come over him since being

lost seemed greater than ever this morning;
he was more and more miserable every minute; something stirred in his troubled mind
—something that told him to travel and travel
until he found the kind of surroundings he
wanted.

He could have gone in any direction; back
over his old trail, off to his right to the open
range, toward the creek again or straight
ahead through the timber. His first move
was a bad one. He walked through the woods
to the open range. Before him lay a broad
valley with high hills beyond. Feeling a desire to take to the open, he walked out as far
as a sandy draw.

He drank from the little run in the draw
and looked around the place. A sudden fear
of this open space came over him, and he trotted briskly back to the woods again to re-
sume his course down the stream. His
prompting was good here, for he had not
been out of sight in the forest more than a
few minutes when three gray wolves swept

across the valley and stopped to drink, a few rods from the place where he had stood.

Trueboy held steadily to his downward course through the timber, sometimes making little detours away from the stream, sometimes moving in still wider circles, but he moved steadily in the same general direction; that was along the low valley where the Little Pine hurried with its waters to the Big Pine River. On Trueboy traveled toward this junction of creek and river—a place where in early May there were cool, quiet waters and rank, lush grass; a place where a wild mallard duck made her nest and reared her young; a place where minnows darted in shoals in the shallows on broad, sandy levels, and more than all, a place where Dan Hudson often came.

Chapter VI

DAN

IT was early one morning a week later at the mouth of Little Pine Creek. The sun had just peeped up from the crimson east to flood hills and valley with smiling amber and the streams with shining silver.

A green stretch of willows bordered the margin of the river here, and many tall cottonwoods, with their fresh green leaves, stood in this favored spot casting a perfect shade on the earth beneath. The place for some distance around was wholly free from underbrush and it was a charming grove for any who chanced to pass this way. Near the mouth of the Little Pine and close to the small bending willows, two mud-hens were swimming and diving and shaking their tail feathers in the joy of the early morning. On the other side of the mouth of the creek a wild mallard mother duck was swimming near some rank grass, where she came each spring to nest and rear her young. A little distance up the river where an arm of willows reached out on a sand bar, a lone blue heron stood, almost concealed by the green foliage around him, making a breakfast on the minnows that came darting past in shoals through the shallow water.

All was at peace here. Even the Big Pine River itself broadened out in a wide expanse and flowed gently over its level bed with only a quiet murmur to the little willows that leaned over and touched its face.

Suddenly the two mud-hens dived; the mother mallard swam quickly out of sight among the tall grass stems; the blue heron flapped his slow wings in flight up the river toward the west.

The morning stillness had been broken suddenly by Dan Hudson, speaking to his companionable horse as he tied him to a sapling.

Dan saw gray wolf tracks in the place, and thinking he might possibly bring down one of these pests of the range, he took his rifle from its holster and carried it into the grove ready for action. He passed well through the trees and was almost to the water when he quickly brought his rifle to his shoulder; but the next instant let it fall at arm's length and then, in his surprise, dropped it to the ground.

What he saw was certainly no wolf; but, a little beyond him and down the creek, sitting and turning his head and looking critically, was a little half-starved black pup. At first sight Dan thought of a wolf, but in a flash everything came to him. He had given up hope of ever finding the lost puppy, and now he could scarcely believe his eyes. A thrill surged through him.

"You wonderful little dog!" he said low, afraid that even words in ordinary tones might frighten him. He bent down slowly but without moving forward. "Trueboy, Trueboy, come Trueboy," he coaxed, but there was a frightened look in Trueboy's eyes; he did not move. Things had been strange and dangerous for so many days that he was a little sus-

picious of this strange form. He was afraid,
and yet how he wanted to come closer.

"Trueboy, Trueboy," Dan kept coaxing,
then patted his knee in token of absolute
friendship. This was the winning stroke.
Trueboy flopped down on the ground and
barked; turned his wise little head to one
side and looked at Dan as if he were saying:

"I am persuaded. I want to come so much
if I could be sure things are all right."

Then doubting a little but believing much,
Trueboy started slowly, then came faster until
he rushed up and leaped upon Dan and
barked and whined, and showed from the
depths of his puppy soul how glad he was.
He licked Dan's hands while Dan petted him
and examined him and talked to him in a
low voice. Dan pulled a mass of leather
strings from his pocket, from which he took a
long leather strap. He fixed this around
Trueboy's neck, and picking him up, carried
him to his patient horse, Dick, who took
things as a matter of course when Dan

mounted with the dog in front on the saddle.

When Dan reached the ranch house his father had already left. Jim Howard, the ranch foreman, and a half dozen of the men were just starting away on their horses for the range, but they dismounted at once to pay their respects to the pup. For a dog on a ranch, and particularly a pup, has a sure place in the hearts of the men.

"Wasn't I lucky, Jim?" said Dan, positively glowing. "I found him in the woods up at the mouth of the Little Pine. He's half starved but I'll soon fix him up. He sure must be a battler to have lived as long as he has."

Jim Howard sat on his heels and after stroking Trueboy and looking him over critically, he said, "Dan, you've got a great dog in this pup. Why, he's going to make a regular elephant of a dog!"

"Maybe he'll kill the Old Roarer," said Dan, half jokingly.

"You keep him close to you, Dan," said one of the men seriously. "Don't let yourself think he can ever kill that wolf. We'll all help you watch him. Keep him at home."

"That's right, Dan," said Jim Howard, moving away to his horse. "You know what's happened to the best dogs Phil Bentley ever had, and to all the other dogs that they've set after the Roarer. You make Trueboy learn that he's got to stay at home and do his romping here."

"Sure," agreed Dan with decision, "I won't take any chances with him. I'm going to make him sleep beside my bunk every night."

The men rode away. Dan, after giving Trueboy food until he was afraid, as he said, that he would "bust," left him in charge of Pete, the good-natured cook, and rode after the men toward the distant herds of cattle. But all through the day his mind was mainly on his new-found dog.

Chapter VII

TRUEBOY BEGINS TO GROW UP

WHILE Dan thought constantly of his dog there was never a day that he did not think of the big wolf, and there was never a day that he did not hunt for him. The late spring and early summer days passed delightfully for Dan and Trueboy, and Dan kept his word—he trained his dog to stay at home.

At the end of June, when Trueboy was five months old, all the men saw that he was going to make a great and powerful dog. His intelligence, as Jim Howard put it, was near to human. And certainly, Trueboy's surroundings helped him; for a naturally intelligent dog that is raised around sensible men with a good master like Dan Hudson, has a far better chance to learn human ways than an unfortunate outcast, intelligent though he may be, whose whole life is a series of kicks, and battles with other dogs.

TRUEBOY GROWS UP

One day Dan's father stood looking at True-boy for some time. Suddenly he said, "Dan, Trueboy seems like a chameleon; his looks change. At times when he's a little distance off, standing and looking at me with his ears erect, he looks like a great Dane; when he turns his side to me he looks like a wolf hound, but when he comes up to me and lays his ears flat and smiles, his eyes make me think of nothing but collie. I guess Bill Henley was right about his breed—he's a mixture of all three."

When the July days came on it was notice-able that Trueboy was developing a great, rangy build. His legs were growing big and powerful, but long; and in spite of his big appetite he never grew fat, but was all bone, muscle and sinew.

Dan and all the men tried hard to teach Trueboy to stay at home, but in this he was like a healthy little boy with a splendid, elas-tic conscience!

Every day after Dan and all the men were gone, and Pete was in the cook house singing

at the top of his lungs and banging his pots
and pans about, Trueboy, too, got busy. He
would walk half guiltily about the premises
for a time, sniffing about the horse corrals,
probably to make sure that no one but Pete
was at home; then he would set out down the
valley and chase birds until he was tired. He
would then begin to investigate everything
near him. Sometimes in going a hundred
yards he would stop as many times to sniff
and smell every bunch of grass; every bush
and scrub tree; every hole in the ground; then
the flat stones at the base of the nearest hill
would come in for a close scrutiny. He came
into the world not only with vast health but,
if possible, with a vaster curiosity; and the
bigger he grew the more curious and restless
he became.

When Dan rode home at evening, Trueboy
was always there to greet him, and such a
greeting! He would leap upon the patient
horse, Dick, before Dan could get off; and
when he did get off Trueboy would almost
knock him from his feet while trying to lick

his face. Dan in exasperation would say, "Get down, Trueboy! Go away until I put the horse away. You've got the roughest 'Howdy do' I ever saw." But Trueboy paid little heed and kept up his antics until Dan unsaddled his horse and turned him into the corral.

Then came one of the "tears" that became the chief feature of the day for all hands. Dan would get an old piece of canvas and he and Trueboy would have it out while the men looked on and laughed and shouted when Dan was all but jerked from his feet; for tall and strong as he was for a boy his age, Trueboy pulled him about in an amazing fashion. Often Pete, meat fork in hand, would leave his cooking to stand outside and look at the fun. Sometimes he would forget all about supper until one of the men sang out, "Pete, you're burnin' that meat again! Even Trueboy won't eat it!" Pete would rush inside, and chuckling to himself, turn his scorching meat.

But these safe, uneventful days could not

last for a dog of the unusual strength and curiosity of Trueboy. It was as natural for a dog of his make-up to be called to range widely as it was natural for his appetite to tell him to eat. It was not that Trueboy did not get sufficient exercise, for he was never chained; it was simply that the wild range was calling him—calling with something irresistible—and always calling him farther away— much farther than the adjacent valley where he ran birds, and the hill where he sniffed under the stones; farther, much farther than this. No one seemed to realize that Trueboy might at any time set out on a dangerous, wild ramble alone.

Chapter VIII

THE STORM

As a rule the first week in August is late to search for young crows, but Dan had already been successful in finding them at this season; shortly after having seen a lot of crows in the north gorge he decided to try again. It was fifteen miles to this gorge—too far, Dan thought, to take Trueboy. He planned, on this morning, to be back early enough to take his dog for a ramble over the near-by valley, and therefore thought nothing more of it when he put him in the cook-house with Pete. Dan talked with Trueboy for a while before he went away; he always did talk to him as if he were human.

"You stay here with Pete," Dan told him. "I'll be back before night."

Dan reached the gorge about mid-forenoon, and immediately saw crows flying and cawing everywhere. He tied his horse at the foot of the gorge and began climbing the tall trees to promising nests. He found half a dozen, but they were empty. He was about to give up, when on coming to a clump of smaller trees up the gorge, he found a young crow on the ground. It could fly just enough to make Dan run to catch it; he captured it and got a real thrill from the great flock of crows cawing excitedly all around him while he put his treasure carefully into a loose-meshed sack. He wandered on up the gorge with the noisy crows still following. A number of owls and squirrels showed themselves but no more young crows.

It was quite late in the afternoon when Dan realized he must start for home at once. A black cloud was coming up with low rumbling thunder. He had been so interested in his search up the gorge that he had not noticed the threatening sky.

He ran down the gorge and got his horse. Dick was moving about restlessly and seemed to be in as big a hurry as Dan was. Dan mounted and the horse leaped forward along the level valley at the base of some high bluffs.

After Dan had ridden a few miles the rumble of thunder was almost incessant; the clouds rolled up rapidly, black and threatening. Dick raced on at a great speed, but not more than half the distance had been covered when the wind and rain struck violently.

It was dangerous to be out in the open in a storm like this, but there was no help for it now. When Dan reached a point within five miles of home he turned his horse across the valley and raced for the ranch house.

The rain drove down in sheets; there came one splitting crash of thunder after another, and the vivid lightning lit the valley like day. Dick splashed through running water. It was one of those dangerous storms known as a cloudburst, and every stream in the vicinity would quickly be a racing torrent.

At last Dan rode in, drenched to the skin and puffing hard. He put his horse away and came into the cook-house. Pete asked him at once if he had seen anything of Trueboy. He had been out calling him for an hour, he said, and had no idea how long the dog had been gone.

Before Dan could reply, Joe Hudson, Jim Howard and all the other men came up outside, with a great amount of noisy shouting to their excited horses, which were rearing and plunging and trying to break away before they could be put into their places. The men came in streaming water and panting and laughing, but when they heard that Trueboy was gone they immediately began to worry. Something must be wrong. He would not stay out in such a storm if he could get home. The places outside were all open. He could not be shut in any of them. Trueboy must be in trouble. They sat up and talked about him for a time but finally, one by one, sought their beds. Dan waited for some time after the men were all asleep, then believing the dog would come in sometime during the night, he left the outside door open and lay down on his bunk.

Chapter IX

EXCITING ADVENTURE

WHILE Dan and the men were sleeping, Trueboy was in trouble. His trouble had begun in the morning a short time after Dan set out to hunt young crows. Pete had talked to Trueboy and paid him attention for two hours or more, then, as the busy day wore on, he forgot the dog entirely. And the truth was it did not seem to be necessary to watch Trueboy any longer. Dan had been away from the ranch day after day, yet the dog had never gone very far.

On this morning, however, as soon as Pete stopped playing with him, Trueboy trotted from the cook-house to begin an intensive search over the premises for Dan. He sniffed around for a little time until he struck his young master's trail. It was so cold that he could not follow it any distance, and he gave it up when well out on the valley. He realized he was free and raced around for the sheer fun of running until he came to the base of a high hill; on up to the summit he ran without a pause. At the top he sat down to look off into strange surroundings. Well in front of him a lone cedar stood painted against the blue haze hanging over the western hills. Above these hill ridges and far to the north and south lay a long blue line of quiet clouds. Far down in the valley to the east near a water-filled draw there came the faint bawl of a calf; this, with a wandering breeze that rustled the stems of surrounding bunch grass, was the only sound that reached Trueboy's ears.

Beyond the draw and some scattering trees far below, lay the Big Sandy and its valley. The Big Sandy was a low, level, wide expanse of sand, at this time dotted with dozens of little pools, with only a very small, shallow stream coursing down through the middle of it.

As Trueboy sat looking into this new country, something about it called him irresistibly. He raced down the hill, splashed across the water-filled draw and came out on the wide level stretches and little pools of the Big Sandy. An hour of thrilling joy he spent here chasing snipes from feeding in the shallow pools. Then, like a boy, he changed his play and splashed in the shallow water after the darting shoals of minnows. Tiring of this, he ran out on the sand bars, seized clam shells in his teeth to toss them and run after them, the while giving voice to deep, laughing barks. But there was so much that was new here, and so much that was interesting and curious that he soon gave up the shells, loped across the bed of the Big Sandy and on to the valley above with its many bushes and clumps of stunted trees. Edging the valley beyond was a long line of shale hills, with here and there long rocky ledges and cliffs.

Trueboy, having forgotten Dan wholly for the time, trotted out onto the level and began hunting around bushes and thickets, working his way eastward to an open grass-covered space, which led away to the foot of the ridges. He was only dimly aware that cattle—many of them—were feeding among the stunted trees and bushes on three sides of him. As yet he had not passed near enough to attract their attention. Instinct told him not to get too close for he was aware that a cow had no love for him.

He covered half the distance to the hill slopes. So far not one of his ancient enemies had noticed him. Suddenly he stopped. He had walked close up to a creature that was at once highly interesting to him, and being in this wild place, it was more interesting still. It was a three-day-old calf lying where its mother had hidden it in a slight depression beside a bush; and it was doing just what its mother made it understand it must do—lie perfectly still while she was away.

Now a three-day-old calf is a peculiar creature. It will lie where its mother hides it, hardly winking an eye, as dutifully as any wild thing that a mother may hide. But if something frightens the calf enough to make

it start up, then there is no young wild creature alive that is capable of getting more
scared.

Wagging his tail, his eyes glowing with
expectation of some kind of fun, Trueboy
stood looking at the little red animal. With
a loud bawl, the calf sprang up and started
running away on its uncertain legs. Trueboy
indiscreetly bounded after it with deep barks
of joy; so interested was he in chasing the
calf that he did not notice the cattle until they
were almost upon him, coming in from three
sides. To make things worse, two young
range bulls charged him hard. Trueboy forgot the calf and ran in the only direction left
—straight for the hillside.

He made the shale-covered slope with the
vast herd swinging in dangerously close behind. He slipped on the loose stones but
scrambled out of reach while the two bulls
bellowed and pawed the gravel below him.
He climbed up and took refuge on a long
line of jutting ledge where he looked out on
the angry bawling mass below him.

[79]

Trueboy did not know that he was mistaken for a big black wolf, ready to kill any of the milling mass below him. He knew only that he must get away. He lay down close to the ledge with his head flat on his forepaws, trying to be as quiet and as small as possible. A miserable time passed in waiting but his enemies showed no signs of going away. He stood up to look for a means of escape and his keen intelligence came to his aid. The ledge extended in a long reach, at some points very narrow, to the shoulder of the hill where the ground fell away on the opposite side to a deep ravine. Trueboy started along the ledge. He threaded his way cautiously; at some points his big, black body pressed dangerously against the cliff when he moved past a narrow space, and once or twice a hind foot slipped off; but he kept on for he was more afraid of the backward course where the two bulls stood on the slope pawing and bellowing their deep angry roars.

He made the shoulder and rounded it, then he slipped out of sight down the opposite side and ran for a mile through the cover of the trees on the margin of the ravine. Here he circled off to his right and trotted leisurely down some gradually falling ground where he found a spot that promised to be a splendid place to entertain himself. This was a long, rugged gorge that dipped for miles back into the hills. The waters of Bear Creek flowed along a tortuous course at the bottom; there were many trees and tall vine-clad thickets and cool, damp nooks that made all odors enticing; and, if Trueboy had wanted any other evidence that the place gave promise, his doubts were dispelled when a cottontail sprang up almost under his nose and raced away with his white cotton flashing.

This small live gray thing was like a racing magnet prickling Trueboy with a thousand tingles and he rushed like the wind, only one jump behind; he never knew how it happened, but he suddenly found himself rushing on after nothing. He whirled; his nose found the trail and he discovered the small, gray, tantalizing thing sitting under a brush-heap. He spent an hour here running around the brush, whining and futilely trying to get the gray ball out, but finally gave it up.

A little farther on, among some thickets, he started another rabbit. Trueboy made an excellent run, turning and dodging with the bunny in splendid fashion; but he suddenly came to grief. The rabbit ran under a seemingly thin obstruction, Trueboy after it, but with a sharp yelp of pain he stopped pushing in and struggled back. The briars had torn his tender ears so that they stung and smarted long after he had reached the clear. Trueboy might have learned a lesson on this morning, which was that in such surroundings it is almost impossible to catch a cottontail; but like all dogs in this matter of chasing rabbits, hope died hard in Trueboy even after his prey had reached inaccessible quarters. Trueboy wasted another half hour here running around the briars and whining and peering in with his eager, flashing eyes. A splash in the water above attracted him and he ran up the stream. He did not discover what had made the splash but this brought him to the shallow water at the edge of the creek, where there were many suspicious holes to sniff. In many of these holes, far back in the darkness, although Trueboy could not see them, wild eyes glowed like two balls of fire and wild ears listened to discover what was happening outside the den. But if Trueboy did not see any of these wild things, his quivering sniffs in these holes told him that wild things were in there; and he was filled with a tremendous desire to come upon some of them as he followed on up the creek. He struck a trail on a level spot and followed it out in the woods until he came to a hole leading under a thicket. Here he began to dig. Sometimes he struck impeding roots which he fell upon with his teeth and tore away. On he worked for an hour with teeth and claws, tearing out a great hole in the earth, stopping to rest and pant and peer with shining eyes into the darkness of the hole. Again he dug and gnawed, and again he stopped and panted. His fine black form was now almost hidden in the deep hole.

When he began to work again, a red fox quietly slipped out of his burrow at the other side of the big thicket and stole away without a sound.

While Trueboy rested again he heard a noise overhead; looking up, he saw a squirrel leap to the branch of a tree high up, and disappear through a hole in the trunk. The sight of the wild thing led him away. He crossed the creek and went trailing up the woods. A wood rat crossed his path; he leaped for it, missing it by an inch, when it darted out of sight under some rotting wood. Trueboy scattered the wood with his big paws and saw only a hole in the ground. No use fooling there, he thought, and he ran on.

Farther on he came to a place where a narrow ravine led away from the main gorge. A peaceful little stream wound its way along here, and for some distance forward the place was bare of trees;—only scattering bushes grew along the stony ground. Suddenly he started up a cottontail and this time the running blood in him had a chance. He raced

and turned and dodged and tumbled the rabbit; it got away again but he was only an inch
behind it with his open jaws when it took
refuge under a peculiar shelter. This was an
old, rusted tangle of barbed wire that had
been rolled down the ravine by many spring
freshets.

Trueboy could see the rabbit crouching
under the tangle; he had come so near his
game he must have it this time, surely. At
first he ran around the wire-tangle as he had
the brush heap; but this time his zeal was
at a high pitch. He whined and voiced a deep
bark.

He began poking his big paws into the
tangle in a dangerous effort to fish the rabbit
out. Certainly, at this moment Trueboy had
forgotten all about Dan. He had forgotten
everything in the world except that he wanted
that rabbit, and he wanted it tremendously.
He stood up on the wire with his front feet
and poked in. His foot caught slightly; he
pulled it out but this did not sufficiently warn
him. He ran around the wire a few times

more and again stood on the wire with his front feet. Again he reached in. He turned to drop on all fours; one of his front feet would not come out. He instantly jerked and then jerked again and yelped a little, more with fright than pain. Still his foot stuck; he jerked hard and violently, but this only seemed to make matters worse.

An odd thing had happened here. Trueboy had poked his foot and leg far down into the wire in such a way that two strands caught in a V shape about his foot while another strand was just in front like a letter A. When he pulled the whole mass of wire the cross of the A tightened down on the point of the V, and he was held as surely as if in a wolf trap. The only difference was that when he was still the wire did not bite in as a trap would have done. But in his fear and desperation poor Trueboy was never still. He fought until he was almost exhausted. While he worked and jerked the mass of wire the cottontail ran out, but he scarcely noticed.

Trueboy thought about Dan now, and sent forth one long agonizing cry after another.

While he struggled the sky blackened with a threatening cloud and the thunder began to mutter. The great mass of blackness came on swiftly, then rolled over him. A splitting crash of lightning shivered a tree nearby, temporarily blinding him. A deluge of rain struck and Trueboy was almost strangled. His most violent struggles were of no avail, but this time luck was with him. Up to this time he had never moved the foot quietly and slowly, but now, hardly realizing his movement himself, he pulled away so gently that the cross of the A did not tighten down and his foot slipped out.

The foot was not much hurt and he forgot it in the storm. He knew now what he wanted to do for he had only one thought— Dan.

Before he had reached the mouth of the ravine the little stream, so quiet earlier in the day, was a raging torrent, and the mass of wire where he had struggled was covered by the flood. It was a long distance down to the end of the main gorge, but fortunately, True- boy did not have to cross either of these two streams. He ran on, keeping under the trees until he came to the point where he had left the hill ridges in the morning. Only his instinct guided him for he ran now in a deluge of rain and the blackness of night. He swung in a wide circle when he came to the hills; then headed straight across the valley to the Big Sandy. How different from the morning when he played over those sands chasing snipes. There was a rushing torrent now. Trueboy trotted back and forth restlessly and whined in his anxiety. He feared to start. But he must get home to Dan. Trueboy plunged in.

The cold, rushing waters swept him down, but swimming was one of Nature's great gifts to him. A pup though he was, he possessed strength far beyond the ordinary dog of his age. He breasted the flood and finally landed, far down on a grassy bank. Pulling himself out with the rain beating down upon him, he stood with his head low, and panted hard. When he had caught his breath he started at a trot and gathered speed as he moved. He covered the last line of hills and ran down into the valley of the Big Pine. By turns he loped and trotted, then, when he must, walked, and again trotted and loped, always splashing in water, until well past midnight, when he came padding wearily in at the door left open, and nosed the palm of the sleeping Dan.

Dan was up instantly. By the light of his lamp he examined his dog and talked to him and lovingly scolded him. And Trueboy whined, and whined, and licked Dan's hands and face, and tried to tell him in his own way that he was miserable and could not understand it all himself.

Dan got up and closed the door, saying, just as if talking to a child, "Trueboy, you will be in this room now every night and the door will be closed. You are too young to be taking these wild runs. If you go away again I may lose you for good."

And as it happened Dan's words were strangely prophetic. Trueboy's troubles had only begun.

Chapter **X**

SIGNS OF THE OLD ROARER

THE warm days of late summer passed, and September came with its soft blue haze over hill and pine.

Every day since Trueboy's wild ramble Dan took him out and endeavored constantly to keep him in sight. But with Trueboy's size and energy this was many times impossible. Trueboy now weighed well over one hundred pounds. He was tall, with big and powerful legs. His short, black hair disclosed his splendid muscles pushing out in beautiful rounded curves; and his four snow-white feet made his appearance very striking. His speed, too, was remarkable.

This was put to a test on a morning when Dan took him to the southeastern part of the range, a region that had not been visited for many days. Out on a level valley a jack rabbit started up. The jack leaped away with a few great "spy hops," using only three legs and with his long ears erect; he seemed to say, "It's just a little morning frolic, nothing more." But he had a surprise coming. Trueboy drove in and Dan, yelling in delight, rode flying after them. The jack was compelled not only to use all four legs, but to lay his ears flat to his shoulders and get down to business. It was as fine a straightaway race as one might wish to see. Suddenly the jack swerved to the right and dashed up a steep hill, on which, because of his short front legs and his long hind ones, he was more than a match even for the best greyhound. Trueboy gave up the chase and returned, panting hard from the swift race.

Dan rubbed him down and said all kinds of flattering things to him, then mounted his horse and rode up the valley. They passed along to the end of the level where the ground dropped away to the bottom of a small ravine, beyond which was a steep, rocky bluff. Trueboy plunged down, crossed the ravine and ran up over the top of the cliff, while Dan let his horse pick his way down the ravine side and up the bluff behind Trueboy. Half-way up the hill, Dick stumbled and fell to his knees, cutting himself on a sharp stone. Dan dismounted, the while condemning himself for putting his horse up the steep place. He examined the cut and finding it not serious walked on, leading his horse slowly up the hill. Arrived at the summit he was about to mount again when he saw Trueboy down in the valley where he had met two coyotes. When Dan first saw the dog he was running slowly with his tail between his legs, as if he were afraid; the two coyotes were running after him to slash him with their teeth. They set upon him, but he whirled and guarded himself with his fangs. They were big coyotes and they meant danger to him. They rushed him hard and slashed him with their cutting fangs, but they began to see that they had more than they expected. Trueboy whirled; he rushed, and snapped, and drove in so fiercely that one of them gave way. The

other quickly followed, but it was compelled
to whirl time after time to protect its rear.
They increased their lead in spite of all the
angry Trueboy could do. Badly scared, they
were running for all that was in them when
Dan came riding down, shouting encourage-
ment to his dog. Trueboy gave up the chase
and came back panting to Dan, who had dismounted and stood waiting to examine him.
The coyotes had given him a few cuts, but
Dan believed they had received worse ones
themselves. "You're a regular battler, old
boy, but you must learn to stay near me—
you're still a youngster," Dan said, as he
mounted and rode on. "There's far greater
danger to you than coyotes, Trueboy—that's
the Old Roarer." But Trueboy only looked
at Dan and wagged his tail, which meant that
he did not understand but that no matter, if
Dan said it, it was quite all right.

They passed on over the rolling valley until
it suddenly dipped into a wide level expanse
covered with stunted trees, with here and
there a water hole. Trueboy, trotting several

yards to one side, suddenly attracted Dan's attention. The dog stopped; sniffed, and growled low. Dan came up to the place and was immediately all interest. He dismounted and bent low over the large footprint of a wolf in the muddy ground near the water. It was the old tell-tale track—one twice the size of the ordinary timber wolf and one that Dan and every cattleman on the range instantly recognized. The tracks were those of the Old Roarer and Dan could tell that they were very fresh, perhaps not more than an hour or two old; in fact it was easy to believe that the giant wolf might have passed the place and stopped to drink in the past half-hour.

Trueboy, sniffing and throating a low, deep growl; the hair erect on his shoulders, his ears laid back to his head, wagged his tail when Dan came up. When Dan made him smell the tracks again, he began to growl again and it was plain enough that he bore this beast a deadly hate.

"He's the one, Trueboy," said Dan, looking almost with awe at the tremendous track in the mud. "That fellow and those that follow him wouldn't leave a bone of you if they ever found you alone."

With his rifle in his hand, Dan led his horse, and walking slowly, followed the tracks for nearly a quarter of a mile along the water holes. Sometimes he missed them, but again picked them up on some muddy ground or a patch of sand. On the grass land he again lost them but persevered, still walking slowly and searching until he found them in some wet sand at the bottom of a draw. Here he was able to keep them in sight for another mile. The draw ended suddenly in a "jump-off" about three feet high. Dan mounted and rode around to the upper ground where the draw first dipped into the valley. There was a wide area of sand here—perhaps a quarter of a mile wide and twice as long—that ended beyond in a sharp-rising hill covered with bowlders and stunted pines. On this sandy level Dan again found the tracks of the Old Roarer, and also what he finally made out to be those of five other timber wolves. The story told by the tracks was that the small band had met here and followed the notorious old marauder.

Trueboy walked slowly beside Dan, sniffed the tracks and growled low with the hair standing on his shoulders.

Slowly they followed the tracks until they came to the hill; here they lost them. It was impossible to find them in the blanket of small loose stones and rocky soil that covered the hillside. Dan gave up trying to track any farther. He rode down to the level and on for half an hour until he rounded the base of a hill range. This finally led him to the point where the Little Bobcat Creek emptied into Big Pine River.

The Big Pine here, and for miles below, was a restless stream. It flowed over great black rocks, between high walls of jutting cliffs, with here and there great fissures filled with earth where a gnarled old cedar clung to life with half its roots hanging free in the air.

Dan stopped here and hobbled Dick so that

he was free to eat the dead buffalo grass. Feeling hungry himself, he took from his pockets some sandwiches and shared them with Trueboy. He ate his lunch slowly and in silence. His mind was on the change that within two weeks he and Trueboy would be making. Joe Hudson and all his men were to move, for this winter and possibly the next, to the Brown Bear ranch many miles to the north. The cattle had already been driven from this range and the scene of chief activity would for a time be shifted to the Brown Bear. Dan was no stranger to these moves. He knew they were necessary for the work of the range but the truth was, as he sat there and looked across the Big Pine River, he was loath to go; for of all the spots he had ever known he liked the valley and hills of the Big Pine best.

Finally he arose, patted Trueboy on his massive head and said, "Trueboy, we're going to leave these parts before long—for a year and possibly two years. But we're coming back. We always have come back, and we may come back within a year. You don't mind going, do you, Trueboy?"

The big dog looked searchingly into Dan's face and barked; it was a deep, roaring bark. "All right, Trueboy," Dan told him. "I ought not to be talking in puzzles to you but your bark is wonderful—as deep right now as the Old Roarer's."

These things Dan said as much to himself as to his dog, and as he rode down the valley toward the ranch house with Trueboy hunting a short distance ahead, the thought of Trueboy's wild night ramble came to him with something like a shock. It would be a calamity to lose the dog now.

"I must keep him close at home until we go," Dan decided mentally. "I'll take him out for a short run every morning and chain him up for the rest of the day. There's no telling, he might take a notion to go on a ramble again."

Twice, while riding near the outer fringe of the Big Pine woods, Dan had to call loud and long to bring Trueboy out of the forest.

Strong and powerful as he was for a nine months' dog, Trueboy lacked experience; he did not know that in hunting he might be in danger without the slightest warning; that a thing that seemed scarcely worth noticing might have in it a deadly peril.

At Dan's loud calls Trueboy came bounding out of the forest, and with perfect willingness went racing ahead toward the ranch house.

Chapter XI

THE last day and night of the stay on the Big Pine brought two unusual happenings. The first was that Dan was so busy he did not unchain Trueboy and take him out for a run of several miles as he had done heretofore. The other thing unusual was the failure to see that a door was closed and latched.

When night settled down over the valley, Dan went out and brought Trueboy in. If he had chained him to the bunk the other things would not have happened, but Dan had been keeping him in by a better way—simply closing the outside door.

Trueboy was restless, and Dan remembered he had been chained all day. He took him out, and followed him around for perhaps twenty minutes, then he called to him, saying, as the big dog came up,

"We'll go in now, Trueboy; you'll get plenty of exercise to-morrow and two or three days later."

Dan brought him in through the middle door of his dimly lighted room and saw to it that this door was securely closed. Then being very tired from the work of the day, he dropped down on his bunk and began undressing. With a sleepy yawn he looked casually across to the outside door on the opposite side of the room. It was closed and he was glad of it for he was too sleepy and tired to walk across the room if he could avoid it. He tumbled into bed, and Trueboy as usual lay down on his coyote rug beside the bunk.

Almost immediately Dan fell asleep, but Trueboy did not curl up and close his eyes as he usually did. His head was up; his eyes wide open. His insufficiently exercised muscles called for action. There is nothing a big dog craves more than running exercise. It urges him, pulls him, and will drive him to strive for it as he will strive for food when he is very hungry. Trueboy, moreover, in spite of his one hundred and twenty-five pounds, was still a pup. He did not have enough judgment, therefore, to resist the temptation to ramble. Dan had not been asleep ten minutes when Trueboy got up and walked toward the outside door. It was seemingly closed, but not closed quite, for the space of a half inch let in the fresh, frosty air. Trueboy put his nose to the edge of the door and shoved it open a little, then pushed it with his paw, and it swung wide. With ears erect and eyes glowing, he stood for a time looking out into the still, moonlit night, then finally turned, walked back to his coyote rug and lay down. But he was very restless and could not seem to get into a comfortable position.

He got up again and sniffed at Dan's chaps and boots lying on a chair at the foot of the bunk, then turned and looked at Dan himself. He wagged his tail and whined low and a little anxiously; but Dan, boy-like, slept soundly through it all.

Once more Trueboy went to the door and looked out. The moon was flooding the val-

ley with a strange, alluring light. He slipped
out and trotted across the level to a near-by
hill; ran up to the summit and sat listening
and looking to the north. An unusual rest-
lessness for the vast open spaces had come over
him. Suddenly his muscles stiffened; the hair
raised on his neck, and every muscle in him
tingled. Far to the north and faint, yet plain
enough, he heard the deep roar of the big timber wolf.

Trueboy sat for some time looking and listening. With a low, deep growl he trotted
down the hill; crossed the level, and came
back to the ranch buildings where for a time
he occupied himself sniffing around the premises generally. Then for the first time in his
life Trueboy set out for a hunt in the night.
There was no direction that called him in particular—he simply wanted to run anywhere
and investigate everything he saw. This sudden overwhelming urge came over him when
he was a short way out on the valley south of
the buildings. There was a clear field ahead
of him toward the south; he headed in that di-

rection. If he held to this course it would in the end bring him into some of the heavy woods along the Big Pine.

In the northwest there lay a great dark cloud, a sure warning that a cold storm was coming before the morning. It was at that season of the year when clouds meant cold and likely snow. Any night winter might fall. The cloud, however, meant nothing to Trueboy. He was well-fed, big, and powerful. His one hundred and twenty-five pounds put confidence into him and he felt quite capable of taking care of himself; but unfortunately he did not know that with all his size and power there were others yet more powerful and dangerous.

Trueboy had set out for a good time and he began having it as soon as he started up the valley. He raced for a time over the withered grass, and at the end of a mile slowed down to an irregular zigzag in his minute investigations of every water hole, bush and stone.

Suddenly he scented game just ahead of

him in a patch of dead grass. He was within a dozen feet of the place when a cottontail started up; turned sharply to the left, and made for the woods. Trueboy raced for it; seized it; tumbled it, and lost his hold; recovered himself and tumbled it again; but once more the fur flew and the rabbit shot into the thickets of the woods with Trueboy reaching for its tail. Trueboy crashed into a thicket but his game was gone. He might as well hunt for a pin in a straw pile as to search for the rabbit in the darkness of the woods. He gave it up to rush quickly on, for the incident had stimulated his desire to hunt.

There was a tang in the frosty air of the wild forest at night that sent every power within him vibrating. He raced through the woods with loud, snorting sounds, thrusting his big muzzle into holes in the ground, and into any promising bushes. Sometimes he stopped and listened; again he rushed on with nose and eyes hunting living wild things. Once he stopped in a broad splash of moonlight, one foot raised like a pointer dog, every muscle in him tense. He thought he heard an animal running through the woods above him. Time after time he started up rabbits only to lose them quickly in the deep shadows. He was giving no thought to the direction now— only running and hunting free and wild as his ancestors had done thousands of years before.

When he stopped and listened the forest seemed to be full of strange noises, yet only for the briefest time were the sounds in the same place; and his instinct made him understand that there were wild things hunting and hiding all around him. Sometimes he heard a twig snap, then he would stop and listen; sometimes there came a faint rustle in a thicket beyond him, but the sounds ceased almost as soon as he heard them. Once he was startled by the breaking of a dead limb above him that fell to the ground. He looked up, but could see nothing in the dark shadows of the tree. He sniffed the fallen limb and went on. Farther along he came out on a point where his feet pressed a covering of fine, loose stones lying in a space clear of trees and brush.

The level, stony place ended at the sloping side of a gorge.

Trueboy crossed the bright, open space and worked down the incline of the gorge around small trees and low bushes until he reached the bottom where a stream coursed its way toward the river. He drank his fill of the cool, fresh water, then trotted on down along the margin of the stream. Suddenly he heard a loud splash in the water ahead of him. He came up to the edge of the creek and found a beaver dam. This interested him and he nosed around the dam for some time, but after the first splash he heard no more signs of life. A little farther on he found himself out of the gorge and in the forest again. He turned, and hunting still, headed toward home.

Moving wherever a scent led him, he walked near enough to the river to hear the sounds of the water. It attracted him; he came nearer and stood on the rim of an incline that dipped sharply to a space bordering the stream. The river at this place ran in a narrow channel for several miles between high rocky cliffs where the water churned below. Trueboy walked down and stood near a rocky bank. Below him the angry waters rushed and swirled over the black rocks of the dangerous rapids, but Trueboy was only mildly curious at the rush and roar of the water.

The point where he stood, and for a distance around, was a level barren place on which wide flat stones lay very plain in the moonlight. A mantle of frost covered the rocks and all the open space around. On the other side of the river there loomed a dark forest. Trueboy pointed his nose slightly upward and sniffed the air toward the river. A small cloud floated over the moon, bringing darkness for a little time, but it passed and the moonlight came again.

A sudden feeling that he wanted to go home came over Trueboy. It was so strong he forgot everything else. He started at a swift run in that direction.

Chapter XII

THE RIVER

WHEN he came into the more open spaces of the forest Trueboy ran rapidly, but some· times he was compelled to move slowly because of tangled vines and brush. His mind now was in a different state from that when he set out to hunt. He paid no attention to sounds on either side of him and would not have run for any small game if it had started up in sight. He saw nothing but the forest and thickets for half a mile, then he was brought to a sudden stop and stood stiff in his tracks.

On his left there sounded the roar of the big timber wolf, startlingly close. His instinct told him which way the wolf was coming, and Trueboy ran straight away down the river. But again he stopped. The hunting cries of four or five other gray wolves

sounded from up the river as they came running down the stream to join the Old Roarer.

Trueboy stood near the river with its high,
steep banks. There was but one way to run
now to escape the enemy. This was to the
right. He leaped away in this direction. He
was too late. The Old Roarer had already
scented the dog and came driving in upon
him. In desperation Trueboy swerved and
ran up the stream and again tried to cut in to
the right, only to be turned back by another
wolf. But his terror of the big wolf drove
him into a battle with the smaller one. It
slashed him; Trueboy gave way, but slashed
it fiercely in return. He leaped into the clear;
crashed into a thicket and out again, but the
pack rushed him hard. For a second he stood
on the verge of one of those treacherous bends
of the high banks of the river. At the edge
he fought desperately; sank his fangs into the
foremost wolf and the next instant the two
were hurtling over the bank. The wolf
struck a sharp rock, tumbled off into the rushing water and disappeared. Trueboy fell into

the water where it churned and beat upon the rocks and lashed so fiercely that it seemed no living thing in its grasp could long survive. He came up half strangled and dazed, but kept on struggling although he was thrown and tossed and beaten until he was only half conscious.

From sheer instinct he still fought on. Once he got his forelegs over a rock and for a brief instant held on, but he was lashed away as if he had been a chip in the angry waters. Half the time he was under the water but still he fought chokingly on. Then, with a final demon-like race, the mad waters threw him out of their grasp into a quiet long stretch below, but on the opposite side from where he had fallen in.

He swam slowly to the rocky shore and crawled up on the gravel and stones. He lay for a time panting hard, but at the end of a half hour he was himself again. He got to his feet and took in the situation around him. He knew he was on the wrong side of the river but he hesitated to breast again the dangerous,

rushing stream. He walked for a long distance down the low shore; looked again and
again at the opposite side, but saw only high
frowning cliffs. It was light enough so that
he could see very clearly for the moon was
still shining. There seemed to be no way
across, yet the courageous big dog would not
give up.

Trueboy moved down the low, almost level
margin of the river and still looked anxiously
across to the other side. Finally he came to
a place where the stream narrowed consider-
ably. He took the chance here and plunged
in. There were no rapids at this point, only a
deep, swift flow, and Trueboy breasted the
current with ease this time for he was a powerful swimmer. He was carried well down
and finally made the opposite side, but made
it only to be disappointed. He swam along
the base of the cliffs trying in vain for a footing. Again and again he tried the shelving
rock at the base, but each time he had to swim
on down and search for a landing. Once he
got clear, but there was only room enough to

stand on the slippery rock where the cliff towered high above him. He slipped back into
the water, tired and panting hard. On he
swam down the treacherous river in his search
for a place of ascent, but the long struggle
had weakened him; he gave it up and turned
again for the opposite side. Unluckily the
stream was wide and deep where he struck
across.

He was half-way out in the river when his
strength suddenly seemed to desert him. His
shoulders sank, and only his nose and eyes
were out of the water. He fought for life as
he had never fought before. On and on he
struggled; his eyes sank; his nose only was
out—with his last strength he battled; his feet
touched bottom; he moved slowly, very slowly
out on the sandy shore and dropped down at
full length, where he lay panting hard for
an hour.

He had had enough of the water for a time.
He was impatient to get home, but he knew
he must wait. He got up and walked across
the open shore into the woods where he

sought shelter under the low-hanging branches of a big pine.

Once in the deep shadows he began licking his wounds and after a time lay still in an effort to restore his exhausted strength. He rested, but did not sleep; his surroundings were too strange for sleep. Something within him made him understand that in the natural order of things a period of light always follows a period of darkness; therefore, he would lie in hiding and wait for the light to come.

A breeze that had sprung up a little before stiffened and blew with a roar through the forest; at the same time the moon passed from sight and a deep darkness descended. At first Trueboy saw nothing, but in a little time he became accustomed to the dark and he could see fairly well down on the shore below him.

He stretched out once to sleep, and fell into a slight doze, when a sound—he did not know what—awakened him. He stood up listening, then, after turning around two or three times, curled up and lay with his nose pointing toward the river. He closed his eyes for brief intervals, but always strange sounds came that made him start up and raise his head. Now and then an odor came to his nose that made the hair bristle on his neck. These scents were new to him, but they warned him, nevertheless, that his enemies were moving in the forest near him.

Perhaps an hour had passed when he heard a faint sound near the stream above him. It was the sound of something heavy stepping on loose stones, and it continued coming down through the woods toward him. Trueboy was not prompted to run as he had been before, for there came to his nostrils a scent that he did not fear. He was not afraid, but merely curious and somewhat suspicious.

Chapter XIII

In a very short time Trueboy discovered what made the sounds. He saw two forms pass below him in the open, one, that of a dog, the other, a man. The man was the good-natured trapper, Indian John, who was seen by the white men only on rare occasions. Indian John led a solitary life in the forests along the streams, with a single companion, his dog, Wolf; who now, as always, followed him. Indian John was late this night, very late, having come from far up the river; he was in a hurry to get to his wigwam before the coming of the cold and snow which he had known for hours was on the way.

It was a little early for trapping, and some of the furs would hardly be fully prime, but Indian John was always early. A few second-rate or even third-rate furs were far better to

him than waiting and doing nothing for another two weeks. He had been looking after
some of his many trap-sets up the river.

When Trueboy dimly saw the forms passing below him, he was not badly alarmed;
however, when he got the scent of Indian
John, he was suspicious enough to lie still and
not move a muscle. Suddenly the dog, Wolf,
stopped. He had scented Trueboy's trail.
Barking sharply he turned and started up
toward the trees, but at a command from Indian John the dog came back to him, and
without any further pause the two passed out
of sight among the trees below.

Trueboy waited and listened. After they
had gone there was no sound for a time but
the roaring of the wind through the forest.
Then danger threatened suddenly; two animals passed a little below on the open space.
The darkness, and the dimness of the forms
made Trueboy strain his eyes to see, but they
vanished and he saw no more of them. Dull
snaps and the cracking of dry wood, sometimes one much louder than the others,

startled him. He was watching intently when a mountain lion came out of the trees to the left of him and stopped. The great cat raised its head and looked at the place where Trueboy lay. Fiery eyes greeted fiery eyes. Trueboy arose and with warning growls came forth, but the big cat, capable as it was of putting up a terrible battle, used discretion. It ran up a tree to a high limb, where it looked down upon the threatening form of the big dog. Trueboy had not pursued. He wanted only to be let alone, and when he saw the enemy was not going to attack him he went back and lay down.

Another hour passed, then a fine sleet began peppering down through the trees, bringing with it sharp blasts of cold that penetrated to every part of the shelter under the pine. Trueboy shivered. He got up and pawed away the dead foliage, making himself a deeper bed, then lay down trying to keep warm by curling up in a ball. The sleet continued to sift through the foliage, and presently snow came driving in with the sleet.

For hours Trueboy lay shivering, and his sleep lasted only for brief intervals. Almost constantly he was being awakened by some unusual loud blast, or the breaking of dead wood near him. Sometimes he awoke in such fright that he stood up and whined. At last the misery and cold became unbearable.

Trueboy decided to hunt for a better shelter. Moving along for some time without discovering a place that suited him, he came upon a tall, dense, vine-covered thicket; he pushed into the center of this; pawed out a bed among the withered foliage, and lay down to await the coming of morning. This new cover was rather better than the first, yet he was cold and miserable enough while he lay for hours, sleepless, and listened to the roaring of the wind, and felt the hissing sleet and snow as it drove through the vines to fall upon him.

With the first light of morning, Trueboy was up with his mind very certain about what he wanted. First, he wanted to eat and then he wanted to go home. He crept out of the thicket and trotted down to the stream. Along the border was something new to him—a scum of ice covered with snow and sleet. Being thirsty he moved cautiously out on the thin ice, and after jumping back a time or two, when his front feet broke through, he found a solid footing and drank, but drank only a little for he was in a hurry to get home.

As he made his way through the woods, the snow ceased falling, but the wind blew sharp and cold. Snow covered the ground everywhere, and the wintry wind, roaring and moaning through the trees, troubled him. He kept near the stream and looked anxiously across at the opposite side, his mind still divided between food and home; but always the strongest urge was to reach home. Farther on he stopped and looked across the stream, where on the opposite side and less than a quarter of a mile across, the banks were gently sloping, with, here and there, narrow, deep-cut cattle trails leading down to the shallow water.

Here a bad thing happened. If it had not

occurred Trueboy would have swum across at once, but he scented food and following his nose he found a moose bone partly covered with snow under the lee of a pile of dead trees. He started for the bone, but stopped ten feet away. For some reason he thought of the Indian and connected him with the food. A slight warning came to him, but it was very slight; it was not the strong sense of danger that would have come to an experienced timber wolf in a like situation.

Trueboy edged nearer. Another scent came to him. It was the iron smell, but this in itself did not much trouble him. He had been around the smell all his life. It meant nothing to him except that he connected it with the strange man; he feared least what he should have feared most. His chief concern was to get the bone and take it away without attracting the attention of the man. He still hesitated and looked sharply around to make sure the human was not near. There was no sign of life anywhere—only the dull roar and moaning of the wind through the trees.

Trueboy walked forward. He was within two feet of the bone when he was conscious, for instinct warns a dog with lightning-like rapidity, that something gave way beneath a front foot; he leaped, but the steel jaws of a wolf trap held him.

He threw himself forward and struggled, but the thing held and cut with excruciating pain. He bit the trap and sent forth great roaring cries that swept far into the forest. His fright was almost as bad as his pain.

But Trueboy was not long alone. Indian John, coming through the woods on his regular rounds, heard the cries and came up on a run. He could scarcely believe his eyes. Certainly here was no wolf but a magnificent dog. Where he had come from Indian John had not the slightest knowledge; but his only thought was to possess the big dog.

The dog, Wolf, in his prime of three or four years and weighing perhaps a hundred pounds, came in, circling and slashing, but John beat him off, then tried to get near the prisoner; but Trueboy in his desperation showed his fangs. His suffering blazed from his eyes and John had much trouble on his hands. After driving Wolf into the woods he talked quietly and kindly, and Trueboy seemed to understand. He ceased his cries and growls, and whined low when John, with gloved hands, came nearer and nearer, constantly talking and always moving very quietly, until he had stroked the great head. Nothing happened; he took a stout thong from his waist and tied it about Trueboy's neck, never ceasing his low reassuring talk. He worked with greater difficulty in removing the trap, for Trueboy, dog-like, was fearful when Indian John got too near the point of pain. John examined the hurt foot and discovered that no bone was broken. The leg was merely bruised and stiff. Highly elated, he started away with his prize toward his wigwam farther up in the forest. Trueboy rebelled. He hung back and jerked like a fighting bronco, but Indian John kept on coaxing him gently, and by slow stages he led Trueboy on, stopping when the big dog sat down and said by his actions he would go no farther; and then again by pulling gently and still talking, he brought Trueboy into camp and there tied him with a long chain to a tree.

Indian John went inside his wigwam to get meat for the big black dog. When he came out, Wolf, wild with jealousy, was attacking Trueboy and a fierce battle was on. John seized a good stick and beat his dog so sharply that he ran off a good distance. "You Wolf!" said Indian John vehemently. "You let him be. He's good dog. You let him be or I whack you hard. He's big wolf-dog. Maybe some day he help you. No more fight him. Maybe some day we go way up river and he *keel big wolf!*" Indian John tossed meat to Trueboy and talked to him while he ate. The injured foot, the trapper knew, would soon heal.

While he was eating, Trueboy paid little attention to the man who was feeding him. Suddenly John said, "Nice Boy—you good boy." Trueboy stopped eating and looked up quickly. John did not know that he had pronounced the last part of the big dog's name. But Trueboy, like every intelligent dog that knows his name, was tremendously interested. This was not enough, however, and likely if the trapper had struck all of his name, Trueboy would have been much the same. It was plain enough that he had no genuine hostile attitude toward John, nevertheless the dog's manner was dignified, and he merely tolerated this new and strange master. Perhaps the word "boy" uttered unknowingly by Indian John only awakened fresh memories in Trueboy, possibly it made him more homesick.

He was so hungry that he ate all the big meal that John placed before him. The trapper at once set to work with pine boughs to make a shelter for Trueboy. He worked hard and long to make a cover that would protect his new dog from the snow and biting wind. When he had finished he spread an old bear skin on the floor and invited Trueboy in. The dog sniffed a little at the fur, then went in and curled up on it, watching John with half-closed eyes—eyes that told plainly enough that he was in utter misery of body and soul. His shelter was good enough, an excellent one in fact, being open only on the south where an opening was made just large enough to allow him to enter; but neither shelter nor food could comfort him in this place.

"Now I leave you, Boy, till we get back," John said in parting. "I theenk you take care of yourself if sometheeng come along!"

Indian John set forth with his gray dog, Wolf, to run the many traps he had set along the Big Pine River. This unexpected delay in making his new dog a shelter would make him late, but time was of little consequence to him in his solitary life.

The snow was again spitting down in fine, cutting flakes. The sky frowned above with heavy gray clouds, which darkened steadily as the day wore on, and foretold a stormy night.

For some time Trueboy lay inside his shelter. He did not put his head down once, but held it up with that wistful look that never left his intelligent eyes. When it seemed to him that his new master was gone well out of range he arose and looked in every direction. Seeing no one, he ran to the end of his chain, leaped back and struggled with all his power to slip his collar, but the strong leather held. He paced around for a time, trembling and whining low, and often pricking up his ears to look out into the forest.

Three times on that day he struggled desperately to get free, and three times he failed. He gave it up; he would lie inside for a time, then come out and walk restlessly around, whine low to himself and again go in and lie down. Once while he was in his cover he saw the gray form of a lynx padding over the snow a little out in the woods. The animal evidently suspected food was in the wigwam for it crept nearer. Trueboy crouched while peeping through the pine boughs. The lynx was coming up the wind so did not scent him.

It came on for the wigwam, which being open, perhaps told the cat it was deserted. When near the dog's shelter the gray beast stopped as if it were suspicious of danger. Trueboy shot out. The great cat leaped;

Trueboy struck and his teeth found its neck. In an instant the lynx fought clear and ran. Trueboy leaped for it but his chain jerked him over on his back. Trueboy's jaws and face were a sorry sight, but his eyes escaped injury. His instinct was to guard the property of even this strange master.

Carrying more muskrat pelts, Indian John came in about four in the afternoon. When he saw the lynx tracks in the snow and the cuts on Trueboy, he knew what had happened, and the Indian was enthusiastic in his praise of Trueboy. "How you do it, Boy, and he no find your eyes!" exclaimed John. "I never see such dog! You great dog—I take good care you, Boy! I not take maybe t'ousand dollar for you! You hear me, Boy, I make good to you." And then while talking broken English and at times full Indian jargon, Indian John fed Trueboy with the choicest bits of meat; examined him carefully to see if there were any bad cuts on him, and was very glad when he found only cuts and scratches

[128]

on the dog's face and jaws which he knew would soon heal.

"I bet you do it queek," Indian John exulted. "He try to steal my meat, you show heem!"

But through all these compliments, Trueboy maintained the same dignified coolness that he had from the first. He stood quietly when John examined him, but there was no wag of the tail—no sign that he was any nearer making friends than when he was first brought in. He ate quickly of the food given him, and drank long of the water placed before him in a tin pan. He appreciated both the food and drink, but appreciated it only as a part of his natural necessity.

Indian John petted him and talked to him, and finally, with the chain still on him, led him about for a time to exercise. After running two or three times around the camp, he brought him back and again tried for some sign of gladness; but Trueboy was the same; he took it all without outward protest but immediately went inside when John told him he might. And now, well fed and well watered, Trueboy lay down in a comfortable bed to rest; but that far away, wistful look was the same in his eyes as in the first hour when he was made a prisoner and chained to the tree.

Inside the wigwam, Indian John soon had a fire going with the smoke coming out through a hole in the top. He cooked his supper and fed Wolf, who slept inside. John had been minded to put Trueboy in also, but knew if he did he would have no sleep for the fighting.

After he had eaten his supper, the trapper sat for a time by the fire, smoking his pipe and looking dreamily into the blaze. After a time he knocked the ashes from his pipe, got up and came out to see how things were with Trueboy in his shelter. John talked to him kindly for a little, then went back in and wrapped himself in his bear skins for the night. Wolf lay on his bed near the flap that made the door. Trueboy could not see full into the wigwam, but only at an angle through the opening. And for some reason, probably because of the new dog, Indian John did not close the flap of the teepee.

In spite of Trueboy's misery, this gave him a slight comfort for he was made conscious that he was near a human, and near one that, while Trueboy did not know or like him, was kind to him at least.

Only the edge of the fire was visible as Trueboy lay and watched it with wide open eyes. Time passed but he did not move; only the fire changed and flickered; at last it burned down to glowing embers. The wind came stronger, roaring through the forest, while the night fell black in the woods.

Trueboy lay with shivers of cold running through him, and memories surging through his brain—memories of Dan—always of Dan. And so, at last, fitfully dozing and dreaming, dreaming that he was again back on his coyote rug; awakening and dreaming again, he lay and waited while the cold wind roared through the trees and the night wore on.

Chapter XIV

FREEDOM

IT snowed in the night but when morning came the air cleared and the wind softened down to a gentle moan.

With the first light Indian John was up. Trueboy saw him do the things on this morning that he did every morning. He first stirred up the fire and threw wood upon it until the sparks went crackling upward. He then fed Trueboy and Wolf, for John's saying was always this: "I feed my dog first; I eat afterward."

A little later while John was eating his breakfast in the wigwam he heard quick snarls and growls outside. He guessed the trouble; picked up a stick and ran out. Wolf was rushing in a vicious attack upon Trueboy, but Trueboy was slashing right back and holding his own.

John caught Wolf and gave him a thrashing. "You let him be," he shouted. "No more fight—I whack you again!"

Wolf slunk off into the woods at a little distance and lay down to await the pleasure of his master. The flogging was a good thing for him; it put a stop to his attacks upon Trueboy.

After John had finished his breakfast he went outside and talked to Trueboy for several minutes. He told him to depend upon it that Wolf would not fight him again.

John was ready to go, and seeing the gray form of Wolf lying in the snow out in the woods, called to him and petted him when he came up. He told him how sorry he was to be compelled to thrash him, and after a few more pats, with which Wolf seemed delighted, the two set out together to run a long line of traps down the river.

Trueboy lay still for an hour. He had seen John and Wolf go away like this before so that he knew they would not return for a long time.

At the end of the hour he came out and stood looking in the direction they had gone. He wanted to be sure. He looked far down through an opening on the snow-covered ground but saw nothing except the cold, silent trees, and heard nothing but the low moan of the wind through the adjacent pines.

Suddenly he leaped to the end of his chain, whirled and jerked back with all his might, trying to slip his collar. He struggled until he was utterly exhausted. Like his other efforts these also failed. He lay down, quivering and crying low to himself; he could not endure this thing. He got up and paced back and forth at the end of his chain. Sometimes he would stop suddenly, and with ears erect look out into the forest as if he expected a familiar figure to come to help him. After looking anxiously for some time he would go back and lie down in his cover.

He was lying thus when John came in late in the afternoon. John fed him and talked to him; took him out at the end of the chain for a half hour's run through the woods; led

him inside the wigwam to try to get him ac-
quainted there; patted him vigorously on his
big black shoulders, and, in fact, did all he
could to induce the splendid big dog to "make
up." It was no use; Trueboy stood still while
John petted him, but that was all. He never
wagged his tail; never looked at the man, and
his eyes, half closed, had only that distant,
lonely, homesick look of suffering.

John seemed to understand and yet he was
puzzled. He brought him back to the tree
and snapped the chain in its place. "You
funny dog," he said, "but you mighty fine dog.
Some day you make up with me." With a
final good word John left him and went about
his work of skinning his pelts and stretching
them to dry. He worked not far from Trueboy and now and then looked up to see if the
dog had come out of his cover.

This life went on for five weeks with but
little change in the order of procedure. Wolf
finally became wholly submissive to the de-
mands of his master; he not only did not attack Trueboy again, but many times in the late

evening he lay in the near-by woods and with half closed eyes looked at the big black dog as if in time he might actually feel friendly toward him.

Good luck was with Indian John in these weeks of trapping. He brought in many skunk, mink, muskrat and marten, and one morning he was unusually elated; he got a silver fox.

As these days went by, John would not have asked for any better fortune except in one thing: he wanted Trueboy to change his mind. The big black dog's mood did not change, and although John did his best each day, he knew exactly what would happen if Trueboy ever got loose. He would run away. Not only that—he would stay away. Where would he go? Who owned him? How did he happen to come where the trap was set? These were questions John asked himself many times but could never answer. He settled down to wait for Trueboy to be friendly. Even if it took months, John believed it would happen in

time. He had the fine dog; he would keep
him.

In all this there was one thing that did not
occur to John—to examine Trueboy's collar.
It had held the big dog for five weeks; this
fact alone kept the trapper from giving it any
thought.

One morning John and Wolf set out together very early. It was gray dawn when
they left for an unusually long journey to run
a new trap line up the stream. It was cold;
the wind howled through the trees and a driving snow came down from the north. A bad
day it was, but it was all the same to Indian
John. He forged ahead at a steady pace and
was soon out of sight of the wigwam and all
its surroundings.

In a few minutes Trueboy left his bed and
came outside. Since his first struggle to free
himself there had never been a day that he
had not tried, and tried again. He knew
again that his new master would be gone a
long time. When Trueboy struggled that first
day and failed he only tried harder the next

time. These frantic struggles had helped him in a way he could not know. The result of them was a much enlarged hole where the tongue of the buckle passed through the leather, and by good luck it was one of those leather collars where the holes for the buckle are punched close together.

When Trueboy came out he stood still for a little time, as he always did, to make sure that John had gone for the day. There was no sign of him or the dog, Wolf, and no sounds except that of the wind and the snow driving through the trees.

Trueboy ran to the end of his chain, whirled and pulled back with all his power. There was a dull thump. The tongue in the buckle had at last torn into the next hole. In a flash Trueboy felt the collar loosen and slip. It reached his ears; he lunged back; struggled; fought until he choked, and tumbled over backward—free.

He sprang up and ran as hard as he could for a mile before he stopped, and only exhaustion stopped him then. He stood behind a log, panting hard, while his eyes looked steadily backward to see if he was pursued. There was no sign of this so he threw himself down on the ground to breathe, for he was weak and trembling. He had lost his endurance since that ill-fated morning when he had stepped into the trap; his muscles were soft and weak. When he felt his wind coming back he got up and went immediately to the river a few yards away. It was frozen except for a narrow swift current near the gently sloping bank where he stood. Along this bank there was a strip of ice, perhaps ten or fifteen feet wide, that reached up and down the stream and out to the running water. He walked out a few feet on the ice, looked anxiously up and down the stream for a crossing, but as far as he could see there was only the narrow channel of running water with the border of ice on the near side.

Trueboy had never forgotten that he must cross to the opposite side; and he wanted all the more to cross here because he could see the banks of earth on the other side and the deep-cut cattle trails leading down to the water. Once across, he could easily get up those banks.

Ice was a new thing to Trueboy, but that strange thing, instinct, told him to be careful. He started slowly across the narrow strip of ice toward the open water. Possibly he thought of swimming the channel; possibly he was only curious, but he stepped carefully. Near the water the thin ice cracked, but he was too quick for it and got back to safety. He walked down the stream, keeping close to the edge, his eyes searching constantly for a crossing.

Around a sharp bend in the river where the ice was well covered with snow, a small drift log lay at an angle across the narrow span of water, and in such a way that it looked as if a crossing might be made.

Trueboy crept along, feeling every inch of the ice until he came to the near end of the small drift log. He put one front foot upon it; it did not move, yet something about it troubled him. He was afraid to try, but he must

somehow cross. He whined and whined again
in his anxiety. Again he put his front foot on
the small log, then the other front foot;
slowly he tested it; slowly he moved out on it.
When he was midway, where there was no
chance to leap forward or backward, one end
of the treacherous support cracked the thin
ice and sank beneath his weight.

At the first plunge he sank clear under the
cold, dark water. Almost by a miracle he was
not swept under the ice on the other side. His
head struck the edge of the ice when he came
up but chance saved him; he came out swimming in the open water. He tried to regain
the shore he had just quitted, but the thin
ice at the edge broke repeatedly under the
powerful blows of his front paws while a
swift under-tow carried him rapidly down
the stream.

He persisted in his struggles to get up on
the ice of the near side, but as often as he tried
the thin ice at the edge broke under him. But
a chance lay ahead. He was carried down
against a giant fallen tree that lay from the

bank to a point far out where the limbs were frozen into the thick ice.

As soon as the water swept him against the tree, Trueboy made a desperate effort to get up on the trunk. This was very hard for him to do. He worked and slipped on the limbs for some time until he made it, then lay down on the great tree trunk and panted. He looked back at the shore he had tried so hard to reach; he could easily go there now, but his mind was made up. He was going toward the farther side.

After resting a little he started across. He moved so slowly that sometimes it seemed he never would make it; he worked his way over limbs and around them—this time the footing must be sure—there must be no slipping. To make it worse the driving wind and snow came whipping down, and time after time nearly swept him off his feet. The cold wind whirled the snow in his face; stinging and half blinding him, but he fought to keep his balance and got across where the ice was thick and safe.

He leaped out on the ice to run for the other side, but the wind rushing down in a biting gale swept him off his feet time after time so that he slipped and slid more often than he ran until he reached the opposite side.

With the feel of the solid ground again under his feet, he ran through one of the deep cuts to the level land above, and pointing his nose in the teeth of the wind, ran across the open for a mile. It was a relief to him when he entered a forest along the stream. With this partial shelter from the wind he settled down into a steady trot and this pace he held for more than three hours. As he hurried along he knew it was a strange forest, and every bush and thicket and stump and tree only urged him the faster. At last he fell into a walk and then got so tired he was compelled to find a place to rest.

He stopped beneath a cluster of giant pines and threw himself down panting. In a very short time, however, he was up and going, traveling steadily to the north as his instinct directed.

Now and then a rabbit ran near him, but he paid no attention to it. His whole mind was centered on one thing. On he traveled over the unknown trail until late afternoon. Then his route took him out of the woods, and he saw directly ahead of him, through the wind and snow, the buildings of the ranch on the Big Pine—his buildings—his woods on the left of them—his home. With a little whining cry of gladness he put forth all his energy and ran. Nearer and nearer he came through the driving snow until he saw the outside door of Dan's room. The snow had banked up on the outside and covered the door half way to the top, but Trueboy suspected nothing wrong. Dan was not in sight but Trueboy never doubted; setting his eyes on the door, he ran for it.

Chapter XV

DESERTED

TRUEBOY reached the door; leaped up on his hind legs; scratched vigorously, and whined to be let in. But he heard no sound—nothing but the driving wind and snow. He stood back and voiced his deep bark that might have been heard a mile away. There was no response. Again he leaped upon the door; there came a creaking sound, and the door, imperfectly latched, flew open.

Trueboy rushed in to a terrible disappointment. He sprang upon the bunk, but only a broken saddle, the coyote rug, and an old blanket lay upon it. There was not the slightest scent of Dan to be found anywhere. Something was wrong here—something he could not understand. He rushed outside and began a swift hunt all over the place, but the search failed. It failed because Dan, disappointed as only a boy can be disappointed, after keeping his father and the whole force of men on a four-day hunt for his dog, had given up and gone away with them weeks before to the Brown Bear ranch far to the north. And on that day Joe Hudson had said: "You'll have to give him up, Dan; he's gone away on another ramble and the Old Roarer has likely got between him and home. He's gone the way of other good dogs. Try to forget, and some day we'll settle matters with the old wolf himself."

Still trusting, Trueboy hunted the place here and there, and everywhere that he could think of. He ran around to the door of the cook-house. It was locked. He rushed to the west side where there was a small window four feet from the ground, and hung on hinges so that it might be swung inside during the summer weather. This window was not locked, but pushed shut in a tightly-fitted casing. Trueboy sprang up and his powerful front feet crashed both the glass and the frail frames around them. He leaped again and went through the wrecked window at a bound. But there was neither sign nor scent of Dan. Only the long bare table where the men used to eat their meals, a smaller table on one side of the room, and a crude cupboard in one corner—only these gave any sign that human beings had ever entered the place. In his swift search, Trueboy whined constantly. Once he gave vent to a series of deep half-barks, half-whines that trailed off into a low cry such as a dog will utter when he is in great distress because he is shut in alone and cannot be with his master.

A door leading to a small back room was slightly ajar. Pushing the door open with his nose, Trueboy entered, and seeing a forgotten ham hanging on a nail on the wall he stood up on his hind legs, lifted it down, and began to feast. He spent half an hour eating, but stopped and listened almost as often as he fed. Before he had finished the ham, still hungry, he began to search again.

He left the cook-house in the same way he had come in, then hunted through the stables

and raced around the corrals. Three times he
ran back into Dan's room, hoping each time
that he would find him there, and at last, when
there seemed nothing more he could do he
curled up on the rug and lay listening and
shivering. Nothing happened. He soon got
up. There was a small square opening four
feet from the floor through which one might
look into the next room. Trueboy stood up
and looked through. It was in this room that
the men often used to sit on summer evenings
joking in their rough, good-natured way.
Trueboy saw no men now, however—nothing
but the cheerless room with its deserted bunks
and cold, barren walls. He dropped down
and went outside. Around the place in a
wide circle he ran hunting for a human trail;
once, twice, three times he ran, but the circle
told him nothing. Back again he came to the
buildings and again he ran into the room he
had left that ill-fated long-ago. Again he
whined and again looked into the room beyond. Here the full truth of the thing seemed
to come upon him. He pointed his nose up-

ward and gave vent to a long-drawn, wild, lonely howl, and if ever a dog cried, Trueboy cried that last time in Dan's deserted room.

With the coming of night the wind went down; a little later the sky cleared and the stars came out to shine upon a freezing world.

In the misery of despair Trueboy went into one of the sheds. He was decided on nothing and remained to shiver and look out of the open shed toward the deserted buildings. Finally, hunger drove him back to the cook-house. He sprang through the broken window; got the remains of the ham, and this time finished it all, even to the bones, which he crunched with his powerful jaws and ate. He got out of the cook-house the same way he came in and went back to the cheerless shed. After pawing out a nest for himself in the old bedding he lay down for the night, but his mind was too troubled to let him sleep. He lay still in utter loneliness.

When the daylight finally came Trueboy paid no heed to the buildings but ran across to the nearest woods where he instantly began to hunt diligently for a wild game breakfast. He hunted until noon with no luck at all, but did not pause to rest. The hours of the afternoon passed with him still hunting desperately to come upon something he could eat; the night fell; he hunted hour after hour through the shadowy, snow-covered ground in the woods, but did not catch one thing. He smelled the trails of a few small wild animals but he was not able to follow them far. Some of them got so cold a little after he ran them for a time that not the slightest scent reached his nostrils. Sometimes a trail led into a dense tangle of vines and briers that he could not penetrate; sometimes he tracked a rabbit to a vast heap of dead brush and boughs that was as impossible for him to get into as if it had been so much stone.

The truth was, Trueboy had picked a poor part of the woods for hunting. He had selected it because it was near the ranch—the ranch to which he still supposed Dan and the men might return. But when the third day and the third night had passed here, and he had caught nothing in the adjacent woods but two mice, he knew he must go.

The fourth day he still hunted in the barren woods, but when the fourth evening came he set out under the stars toward a deep, wooded gorge to the north. He came to the fringe of trees along the gorge and stopped to look and listen. Deep stillness pervaded the earth. A white blanket of snow stretched away in every direction for miles over valley and hills. Trueboy heard no sound nor saw any moving thing. He quietly padded down to the depths of the gorge. He had gone but a short distance when a rabbit moved out from behind a rock in front of him. He raced for it, but it eluded him and took refuge in a hole in a rotting stump. Trueboy tore away the decaying wood with his powerful teeth and jaws and in a few minutes got his game.

The rabbit was a good meal for him and Trueboy was again ready to sleep. However, he did not go back to the shed; it was too lonely there. He dug down in some leaves under a projecting ledge of rock and spent the night in the gorge.

For nearly three weeks he spent his time hunting within a radius of several miles of the ranch buildings, going back to them now and then, but each time he shortened his stay and he began to feel that somehow Dan was completely lost to him.

Then came one night, when after a very brief run about the buildings, Trueboy gave the thing up and headed straight away up the valley to the north. He ran for miles without stopping. Midnight found him far up the river near a wide expanse of dense woods. He entered this place to hunt, for it seemed to offer some faint promise. He must eat or die, and must die unless by his own efforts he could get food; his handicap, moreover, in getting food, compared to wild things, was tremendous.

In all of his trouble Trueboy's state of mind never changed. The master he would have risked his life to reach was gone, and yet the big dog was none the less devoted to him. If possible his devotion was all the greater because of his great loss. It mattered not to Trueboy what had made Dan leave him. Nobody in the world could take the place of Dan. Therefore, while Trueboy set out to live alone there was always back in his brain somewhere the memory of Dan and a longing to find him.

But at present his hunger overcame everything; he hunted until three in the morning with no luck. Suddenly, as he came out of the trees to the open range he heard a sound that struck fear to his heart. It was the deep roar of the big timber wolf and the cries of the small pack that followed him. Trueboy stood and listened to get the direction. Twice more he heard the wild, weird cry of the pack, above which came the terrible bass of the Old Roarer. They were heading west a good distance beyond him. Hungry as he was, Trueboy ceased hunting. He spent the remainder of the night moving about the immediate vicinity and listening for sounds of his enemies. When morning came he was ravenous. For hours he hunted in the woods, and by admirable cunning and patience he captured two red squirrels. This was excellent; he was learning rapidly. When the night fell again he sought shelter under the roots of a fallen tree. He slept but little, however, and again in the later hours he heard the roar of the old wolf. Instinct made Trueboy afraid, although he knew that he had great strength. He weighed now, in good flesh, one hundred and forty pounds. He was not yet a year old and was still growing; he would reach at least one hundred and fifty, if not more, when fully grown.

This growing strength of body made him more confident of himself. All he needed was food and every time he succeeded, as he had in the earlier hours, in catching a cottontail, and now and then two of them from sun to sun, he felt the tingle of strength running through him. But in the big magnificent Trueboy was born caution. He knew how near death he had come that night when he ran afoul of the Old Roarer and the other tim-

ber wolves. Moreover, with all his growing
strength, Trueboy knew mighty well that the
big wolf was a constant danger. And Trueboy was wise enough to know that he must not,
on any account, let the huge beast get near
him.

So the time went on, the clear days and the
stormy days; the moonlit nights and the nights
when the biting wind and snow drove down
out of the north to sting and cut with icy
clutch to the bone—and nights when the wind
howled and moaned unceasingly through the
Big Pine forest. As these days and nights
passed there grew in Trueboy something beside caution when he heard the wild night cry
of the Old Roarer. It was a terrible hate, for
in some way he connected these wild marauders with all of his troubles. He never
forgot what had happened on that calm frosty
night, the night that now seemed so far away,
when the Old Roarer and the other wolves cut
him off from home and dashed him into the
dangerous, dark waters of the river. And if
Trueboy was devoted to Dan to the point that

he would lay down his life for him, he was just as much devoted to the everlasting hate that he bore the Old Roarer and his band. There is no greater hate than that which a dog will bear toward one of his kind that had punished him badly. But in all of his hate Trueboy was wise—wise because he was cautious.

Chapter XVI

SOMETIMES after hunting in some familiar gulch or ravine for an hour or so Trueboy seemed to remember that Dan had often been in this place with him. The dog would stop suddenly, with one foot raised, and look quickly in all directions. And as often as he came to one spot in particular, the place where the Little Pine Creek emptied into the Big Pine River, he would sit and look and listen for an hour at a time; then with nose to the ground he would run through the grove making a most diligent search for the lost trail of his master. When he found this to be in vain, he would trot back to a little knoll nearby and sit down to look. There was no point far or near that his eyes did not see. His failure to see only increased his desire to try and try again.

Sometimes, after he had sat for an hour or

more looking from the knoll near the mouth
of the Little Pine, he would start suddenly to
his feet; run a mile across the valley and up to
the top of a high range of hills. Here on
some high point, he would again sit down to
look. Sometimes he remained in this tense,
expectant mood, moving not more than a few
feet, for two or three hours at a time. Nor
did that day ever come when he ceased wholly
to think and look for the friendly human beings to whom his whole life was devoted.
And on many a clear morning his great, dark
form might have been seen on some snow-
capped hill while he held his hopeful, longing vigil. And thus when the spirit moved
him, sometimes by day and sometimes by
night, he got to some high point and looked
into the distance for some sign of those who
had so mysteriously disappeared.

Trueboy had freedom now—more than he
wanted, for it was a vast, wild region where
he found himself.

He hunted for three weeks with no particular place in mind and no particular home

to hide in; but at the end of this time an old
instinct told him, as it tells the wild things,
that he should have a hole or den for his own
—a place where he might always find shelter
from the storms, and if he had fed well
enough, a place to which he might return to
sleep.

With this in mind one afternoon he left a
gulch in the open and ran over the snow to a
long belt of timber which he entered and
passed through until he came near the border
of the frozen stream. He made his way upward through this forest for a quarter of a
mile, when, at a bend in the stream, he came
to an immense drift of logs and brush that
had been left by the high water of the spring
freshets. This drift lay a few feet up from
the ice and there were numerous holes and
dark recesses in the débris that had no snow
in them. After sniffing about the place for a
time, Trueboy crawled into a hole that extended four or five feet back from the light
outside. There were enough fine dead wood
and leaves inside to make him a comfortable

bed. His luck in hunting on this day had been poor, and he was hungry, but he was tired and the den was comfortable. While he lay down with his head up and looked out in the waning light he heard squeaking sounds in the drift around him. To him this meant but one thing—small animals and food. It irked him exceedingly to hear the sounds all around him and yet not be able to see the things that made them. He stood up in the den for some time listening and watching, but nothing came of it.

The small game in the drift kept up such a constant squeaking that it seemed to Trueboy he surely could get some of it. He hurried outside, smelled quickly all around the mass of dead limbs and brush, then fell to work with his feet, and pawed out large holes in numerous places, but while he worked the night fell and he was compelled to give it up. Hunger troubled him greatly, but he went back into the den. The place was comfortable and the promise of food made him decide to wait until morning.

SURROUNDED BY ENEMIES

A fine powdery snow sifted down all night, filling the opening of his den almost to the top. When the daylight came he pushed out through the opening, shook the snow from his thick black coat and stood for a minute looking out over the silent woods and stream. Snow lay heavily on the boughs of the trees; it capped vine-covered thickets and rolled itself into a long spotless cover of shining white far up and down the frozen Big Pine River.

Trueboy set to work in earnest on the drift, and this time he excavated a wide, deep hole and dug deeper and deeper. His paws suddenly struck into a vast pile of nesting material and woodrats ran in every direction; there was a lively time. Trueboy got three of them, leaped and snapped for two others but missed them and started energetically digging for more. For hours he dug and pulled away bits of wood so that when he had finished, half of the drift was scattered about. All the other rats seemed to have gone into inaccessible quarters, and finally, panting hard from his exertion, Trueboy lay down and gave up further attempts.

After resting for a time, he got up and moved watchfully out into the forest where for two hours he hunted with the skill of his growing experience. Trueboy saw nothing, yet in that time he had passed a hundred wild eyes watching him, nor was he ignorant of this fact, for time after time his nose told him there was unreachable wild game in some great hollow log or some large bush. He came out to a point where a long snow-covered arm, several rods wide, reached down from some low foothills into the forest. This arm was barren of trees but thickly bordered by them on either side. Trueboy came up and while standing between two thickets heard a slight scratching sound beyond him. He held steady, never moving a muscle, and in a few seconds caught sight of a red squirrel. The squirrel, in its quick, jerky manner, was coming down a tree at the edge of the clearing. Trueboy made a mistake—he crouched quickly to the ground—the squirrel saw the movement. It ran back up the tree and began a series of angry barks. Trueboy, having crouched, made no more mistakes but lay half hidden between the thickets. For some time the squirrel continued its barks; came half way down the tree, turned, ran up the trunk, and again barked angrily for several minutes. Once more it started down the tree, stopped when half way, looked at the half-concealed form of Trueboy, and turned to run up the tree. Trueboy did not move. The squirrel came to the base of the tree, hesitated, ran out ten feet in the open for the other side, back again and up the tree. Twice it repeated these actions, going a little farther each time across the open toward the opposite side. It came down again and after two or three false starts, ran for a tree on the other side.

Trueboy shot out and caught his game when it was within ten feet of the opposite tree. This would have made a dog of ordinary size a fair meal, yet Trueboy was not half satisfied. He turned back to plow through the deep snow of the forest for several hours, but

[163]

it seemed as if the squirrel had been the only living thing in the woods except himself. Finally he stopped to look and listen for signs of any wild thing. The air was still under a sky overspread with leaden clouds.

Suddenly there was a crashing sound in a thicket in front of him and a deer leaped away. Trueboy did not pursue. He had seen one or two of these animals before and to him they were too much like the cattle—something he did not particularly like, yet something he must let alone. Moreover, he was doing fairly well on small game, and although he never had all he wanted he got enough to keep him hunting, and hunting always for the small things.

He traveled toward the north for a time, then hunted in a wide circle until he came to a point where the heavy forest fell away into a deep canyon. Trueboy started carefully down the sides; worked his way in a zigzag to the bottom of the canyon, and moved with it toward its outlet. At the end of an hour he came out on a broad, level space, dotted

with tall bunch grass which pushed its dead
stems up through the snow. Suddenly his
nose caught the scent of game; at the same instant a jack rabbit started up only a few feet
away. The jack, probably stiff from a period
of inaction, had hardly started when Trueboy with an amazing burst of speed caught it.

Here was a splendid meal, but he had
scarcely started upon it when trouble began.
Two big coyotes, as large as ordinary timber
wolves, had, out of much curiosity, been trailing him down the canyon, when they saw him
seize the luscious jack; they wanted it and
came rushing upon him. The coyotes circled
him with bared, menacing fangs. Trueboy
held his forefeet on his game and snarled
threateningly. One of the coyotes swept in;
Trueboy made a mistake. He left his game;
set upon the coyote and beat it back quickly,
but the other seized his rabbit and ran. The
coyote was a faster runner than Trueboy, but
the added weight of the rabbit was in Trueboy's favor. He finally came up, the coyote
dropped the big rabbit, and there was a short,

sharp battle before Trueboy could drive back the other animal. He turned just in time to rescue the jack as the other coyote rushed for it. This time Trueboy was wiser; he held his game under him and snarled with flashing eyes and bared fangs as the two hungry animals circled around him. But he did not leave his prize to attack them. When they saw he was not to be lured away they gave the matter up; they had had enough of his fangs anyway.

When they had loped away to a safe distance, Trueboy fell upon his feed and finished it, then ran for a mile over the snowy wastes to a rise of ground on which grew many clumps of stunted bushes. Ahead of him he discovered something that made him drop flat in his tracks. Not far below, in a wide depression, he saw the giant wolf and five others following him. The wolves were on a trot and headed for the forest some two miles to the west. Luck was with Trueboy, for the slight breeze that had sprung up was in his favor. He crouched low and waited until the gray wolves had had passed out of sight in the forest; for some minutes afterward he lay still and peered cautiously around the bushes. His victory over the coyotes had in no sense blunted his sense of danger to himself. In his brain, instinct worked rapidly.

The nest that he had discovered in the drift was far to the north. He must not now enter the woods to travel in that direction, because the Old Roarer and his band might be encountered at any point. However, it was in his mind to run a long distance around and come finally to his den in the drift. It was a comfortable shelter; he wanted to pass the night there as he had the night before.

Keeping a sharp look-out in the direction of the forest, he arose and ran at an angle away from the trees. At the end of a half mile he slowed down to an easy lope, came up to a high point on the rim of a hill, and looked back, but there was no sign of his enemies. Again he ran on, this time for several miles, and just as the first shadows of evening were gathering, he entered a narrow strip of the forest and came to the river's edge. He turned back toward the south and the drift heap, keeping close to the edge of the frozen stream.

Suddenly he stopped. A faint sound had reached his ever listening ears. He waited a little, then again moved forward, and again luck was with him for the little wind that had sprung up in the afternoon had died away with the coming of evening. The faint sound once more came to him; he stopped and listened, and again stole forward at a slow walk. From the edge of a bend in the river he peered around a thicket. His drift was below him on the other side of the bend. Instantly he saw what made the sounds he had heard. Digging and working in the drift, where Trueboy had worked in the morning, were the giant wolf and his followers.

Trueboy turned and ran back over his trail toward the north, keeping among the more open spaces in the trees, so that he might make greater speed. All thoughts of returning to the drift were gone from his mind. He ran on and on until the night fell and the stars peeped out dimly to light him on his way. Finally, coming upon another wide bend in the stream, he left the woods and crossed the snow-covered ice of the river. On a long stretch of open, rolling land on the other side, running still and always holding to the north, he finally came to a place where the sides of a rock-studded gorge fell away to the open valley. He crossed the level; turned into the gorge and climbed slowly up one side, making his way around huge rocks, stunted pines, and little vine-covered bushes; sometimes he floundered in a snowdrift, sometimes backed out of a mass of bushes and vines to go around them, and finally, high up under a shoulder of rocky cliffs he found an opening under a ledge of rock. It looked like a good hiding place; he crept in and remained for a time, then went outside and sat on the narrow level rock to look out and down on the valley to the right of him.

While he watched from this high point, the moon pushed up over a long rim of hills

in the east and shone brightly on the snow-
covered ice and level valley to the north and
south. It was long before he gave up his
watch but he saw nothing of his enemies, and
no sound came to him of their wild hunting
cry. Being very tired he crept back under the
warmer shelter of the den, but he did not
sleep. Sometimes he would lay his massive
head on his great forepaws and draw a long,
weary sigh that trailed off into a little quiver.
But that was all. Trueboy made no other
sound. He lay still and rested, but he never
stopped listening.

Chapter XVII

THE moon shone high in the heavens and the night was half spent when in a dozing, dreaming state Trueboy suddenly raised his head in the den to listen.

Faint sounds had reached his ears. He crawled to the opening and pushed outside. On the still cold night came the wild howls of the Old Roarer and his pack. They were headed up the valley with cries that sounded steadily nearer.

Suddenly, out of the dim shadows on the other side of the frozen stream, there bounded a splendid buck. The deer started up from the woods to the south and although he did his best he was not able to increase his lead until he struck a hard rocky ridge farther on. He flew like a shot over the ridge and vanished into the faint outlines of a wood far up the valley.

The big wolf and his pack swept past on the trail with their cries ringing wild in the night. Then faint and indistinct they sounded far in the north, and finally ceased altogether.

Again the night was very still.

Trueboy went back into the darkness of his den and lay with his head up, listening until morning. When he emerged a bright sun was streaming over a vast white world.

Trueboy started up the long, winding canyon toward the west. Some instinct told him that the Old Roarer and the other timber wolves hunted on the other side of the river. There was good reason for him to sense this. He had many times crossed their trails during the weeks of his existence there, and night and day he was afraid that he might run afoul of them. An accident had driven him into the canyon. To him it looked like a good time to leave his dangerous enemies for he thought his latest den was too near the hunting ground of the Old Roarer.

He picked his way down the rocky steep to the bottom. Ahead of him he heard a gentle roaring sound, but it did not frighten him, rather it led him on. He moved forward and came to a giant waterfall more than one hundred and fifty feet high. A great mass of rough ice lay below, where the cold seized the water the moment its movement became slower.

Trueboy worked over the rough irregular ice to a little stream of running water, and drank. There was a wide level space at the bottom of the canyon here where on both sides of the frozen stream grew many small cedars and little clumps of bushes. These little thickets also extended up the sloping sides. Trueboy hunted about for a half hour. He saw nothing until he looked up on a sloping brush-covered bank. Then he beheld a big gray owl, perched on a small bush, silently watching him. Trueboy's eyes snapped with expectation. He tried to stalk the owl by working carefully around the bushes to a point a little above the creature. He succeeded in this and saw the great owl a little below him, facing down the slope. Trueboy started stealthily forward. He was almost near enough to make a rush when the great gray head of the owl slowly turned and the staring, round eyes saw the form of the black dog. The owl flew away down the canyon while Trueboy stood watching it in bitter disappointment.

He made his way up the side of the canyon and around to a point well above the waterfall. He was heading westward because he wanted to find a hunting ground far from that of his enemies.

The canyon was one that pointed westward to a long line of high foothills and grew shallower and wider in its upward course. Finally the canyon ceased and Trueboy was in a region of little valleys and rolling hills. The farther he ran the better he liked the place. He scarcely stopped to hunt but ran for miles over long level spaces where only small round stones pushed up out of the snow. Down sharp inclines he sped and up over little round knolls; across wide stretches of ice-covered lakes; and finally, late in the afternoon, ne found himself in a valley that lay between two high bluffs with its farther end falling gently down to a lower level in the center of which was a small lake, and beyond this was a lovely pine woods. The low hills on either side of this valley were thick-covered with big rocks and little trees with bare patches of ground looming here and there. All this drew Trueboy with a certain charm. The whole locality suited him. He decided to stay.

Up along a shelving hill he climbed until half way up, on the northern slope, he found under a gnarled old cedar a spacious hole. The ground all around the hole was covered with bushes except that immediately in front, which afforded a level space of some four or five feet square. It was what he wanted for a den. He pushed in past some overhanging roots and found a spacious pocket well back in the hillside.

He was tired from his long run up the canyon and after pawing out some of the dirt to make a better bed, he lay down and slept until morning.

With the first good light he came out and immediately ran toward the pine woods at the head of the lake. He had not gone ten yards into the woods when he came face to face with a white stoat. The big weasel, with all the daring savageness of its tribe, stopped when it saw running was useless and faced Trueboy. He rushed upon the killer as if it had been a rat, and ate it instantly. A little farther on he ran upon a weasel running on a hot rabbit trail. Trueboy again feasted.

His luck in getting the two weasels on this first morning was as good as it was unusual. He rushed here and there hunting trails; stopped often to smell in suspicious holes; passed on through the timber and ran in a wide circle over the rolling ground beyond; back to the timber and in this way put in the rest of the day but he saw no more game.

He returned to his den late in the evening, crawled back to the end of the cavity, and lay down to pass the second night.

The next day he made a discovery. He started up a number of cottontails in a clump of woods near a great mass of stones and holes in the center of the level space. Every time a rabbit started up it shot out for the holes under the rocks and escaped.

Trueboy wasted valuable time here. Every morning he came to this vicinity and spent his strength racing after the rabbits. They escaped him many times; in places where day after day he dug after them until his toenails bled, and his teeth stung because he tried to bite away the frozen ground; yet morning after morning with that same determined energy poor Trueboy rushed them into the holes and worked until he dropped trembling and exhausted.

On the fourth morning about the middle of the forenoon he left the holes in the frozen ground to try his luck in a ravine that separated two clumps of woods farther west. He passed through the woods and at the outer edge a rabbit started up. Trueboy rushed the game and there seemed hope of success, for it

ran across the narrow level toward the ravine,
Down the ravine side it ran, going lightly over
the frozen snow with Trueboy pushing close.
Into the dip they ran; the rabbit shot across
the snow and over the tops of some protruding
bushes. Trueboy drove hard but suddenly
while over the frail thicket, his weight broke
through the snow. He plunged through stems
and vines to the ground ten feet below. This
surprise was instantly followed by a flutter all
around him at the bottom of the thicket. He
snapped like lightning and got three grouse
out of a dozen imprisoned by the snow. The
nine whirred away, but Trueboy made a great
meal on the three.

His next business was to get out. He could
see daylight above him where he fell through,
but it was impossible to get out that way.

He walked around under the vines until he
had put his nose into the snow in every point.
His sense of direction was purely instinctive;
he plunged into the soft snow; pushed and dug
and floundered; veered a little, now to the
right, now to the left; surged forward again

with the feel of an upward slope under his feet, and ten minutes later pushed his great black head up through the snow crust and climbed out on the other side of the ravine.

He wandered on up to the level ground and down on the other side into a deep bowl in the hills, the bottom of which was thickly covered with brush two feet high.

Trueboy spent an hour pushing through the low brush in an effort to start up new game but he saw not even a bird in any of the bushes.

All the rest of the day he hunted in this locality, but saw no signs of life except some rabbit trails and these did him no good.

When night came he went back to his den.

Trueboy had succeeded in getting away from the Old Roarer and his pack, but a new danger found him here; he had come into a region where existence even in a moderate winter was very uncertain. Sometimes he hunted for three days and three nights and did not get a bite. At these critical times he would decide to go back into the dangerous territory along the Big Pine, then he would catch a weasel or a rabbit,—once he got a civet cat;—and in this way he stayed.

As the weeks dragged by he grew thin; his once beautiful, glossy black coat was stiff and harsh; he was only the shadow of himself compared to the magnificent dog in the days of plenty. Yet somehow he lived until spring.

Luckily spring days came early. The snow on the southern slopes melted quickly, and gradually the deep drifts in hollows, deep ravines, and overhanging ledges on the north disappeared.

When the bright, warm days of May came Trueboy hunted in the swales and draws with the sounds of murmuring water coming to his ears.

By the first of June he was himself again.

A mile west of his home he found a lake in the center of a beautiful green meadow. The little valley was alive with ground squirrels, grasshoppers, bugs, and a thousand creeping things. Several rods from the lake was a deep bog with small water holes where green frogs came into being as if by magic. These, too, were excellent food and Trueboy lived off the fat of the land. His coat was again a deep, glossy black; his four white feet were whiter than ever; his intelligent, yellowish brown eyes told that he was as keen in intelligence as he was strong in body.

Yes, the place now was a little haven for food; all his physical needs were supplied here. But something was wrong with Trueboy's spirit—something inexpressibly, pitifully wrong.

Many times on a clear night, especially when the moon was up, he would sit on the hilltop above his den and in the cool stillness look away to the east. Only the croaking of the frogs in the swale broke the night stillness. But Trueboy was unconscious that he heard any sound. He was living far from his surroundings in another and distant world with his memories.

June passed and the warm days of July came with the drowsy hum of insects on meadow and hillside. The little streams, no longer troubled by the rains of spring, ran clear and cool over little gravelly beds in the draws and hollows. In the little woods beyond the upper end of the lake the blue jays sounded their lively cries to mingle with the redbird's musical whistle to the morning sun; on the hillsides and the trees of small ravines the crows flew peacefully about, cawing to their neighbors feeding in adjacent grassy fields; out on the green meadow near the lake, meadow larks perched on low bushes and grassy stems, sent forth their clear, sweet calls in the fresh early mornings. Here the skies were always clear, and often on the still evenings a beautiful cluster of small thunder heads lay in the west like a flock of snow-white sheep peacefully sleeping on the shafts of the setting sun.

It was a valley of summer and beauty, but its allurements could not ease the mind of Trueboy.

One night in the first of August he sat on the hill above his den looking away into the east. A feeling of unbearable loneliness had been in him all that day; it grew in him stronger and stronger with the falling of night. He whined anxiously as he sat looking. This was the first time he had given this outward expression of his feelings while looking from this place and it told of his unusual loneliness of soul.

He did another unusual thing. Always before he had been in the habit of sitting still and looking about. On this night he got up from his sitting position, walked nervously around, stopped often to look eastward, and each moment got more and more restless.

Suddenly he started away. He ran at a brisk lope to the east; for miles he sped on and on, over high table lands; down long rocky hill slopes; across broad level valleys; up steep hillsides, and along high winding ridges that lay for miles under vast stretches of shadowy pines; and at last, having taken the shortest route he could, he stood panting by the waters of the Big Pine River. A little back of him was the mouth of the long winding canyon. He had spurned its long torturous course from his wild home and had run almost as straight and as sure as a bird might have flown the entire distance.

Instinct had guided him, but behind the instinct was his love for one human being.

Trueboy was in wonderful condition. He was fully grown, and weighed a little over one hundred and fifty pounds.

For a few minutes he stood looking across the broad waters of the river. He saw no movement in the valley beyond and he heard no sound.

As to the wide, deep waters, they were nothing to him. He plunged in and breasted the stream with his mighty chest. Swiftly he swam, making the grassy bank on the other side with no feeling of fatigue in his great body. He shook himself, throwing the water from him in a fine spray. Down the valley he headed, making straight for the big rounded circle of timber several miles down the river. He ran over the level valley at a gentle lope, watching constantly in front of him and on both sides for big moving forms;

listening with ears keyed high for near or far
distant sounds, and thinking constantly of the
wolves whose region he knew he was now in.
He stopped—but he had heard only the deep,
buzzing sound of a night hawk—he ran on.

As he approached the wide, dense woods he
circled far to the east; leaped up the hillside
to a ridge, and followed it for two miles;
then dipped down into the valley again
and hurried, believing and doubting, to the
ranch buildings of other days.

The dawn was creeping in when he arrived.

The place was as he had left it except that
the green grass and white wild flowers grew
up to the very doors.

Trueboy went into Dan's room. It was
empty as before. The coyote rug had been
dragged into a corner; tussled with; chewed,
and torn by some animal. Trueboy got the
scent, drew back with a rumbling growl, his
eyes flashing a deadly fire.

Outside he came with hair bristling like
mane on his shoulders; the wild deadly light
in his eyes. Moving slowly and watching the

corner of every building and shed, he searched the place in the gray light of morning.

By and by he crossed the space between the cook house and the north corral, and with nose to the ground passed around to the east side of the corral. Deep in the soft mud beside a small water hole he came upon the tracks of the Old Roarer. The same scent was here that was upon the coyote rug. The trail was less than an hour old.

Trueboy threw up his head and looked north. The wild gleam was in his eyes; the hair stood stiff on his shoulders, but caution, that thing in him born of the highest intelligence, never left him. Dan was gone utterly; the big wolf himself came into the place when he would. Therefore, this was no place for Trueboy. He had come with a half hope, but he had found it worse, miserably worse than he had supposed. The place was forever deserted by Dan and all men. He would leave it now—leave it, like them, forever. His mind was made up.

Trueboy selected his return course up the valley with the same wise caution he chose in coming down. If he could prevent it there would never again be a time when the giant wolf with his pack would come upon him unaware.

In due time he reached the Big Pine River directly across from the mouth of the canyon. He plunged into the stream immediately and crossed over. A feeling of greater safety but one of most bitter disappointment possessed him. He did not care for the shorter route over the highlands—nor did he care to hasten on the return trail. The wild gleam left his eyes; they were half closed as he walked along listlessly and with no attention to any of his surroundings.

The sun arose to shine down on the cool depths of the canyon; the crows flew slowly over him, cawing a warning about him to one another; the bluejays scolded with their harsh cries, but to all this he was oblivious. Slowly he wandered on, walking with head hanging low and eyes without luster or interest.

It was night when he reached his den. He went in and lay down, drew one deep, quivering sigh and was still.

When Trueboy came out the next morning the bright warm sun was streaming over the hillside.

Feeling comfortable in the sunlight, he sat out on the space in front of his den to enjoy himself merely by looking around. As he turned his eyes toward the lower slopes, he saw something that sent a thrill of pleasure surging through him. It was a mother coyote leading her young, to the number of nine, down a gently sloping, grassy hillside. The little coyotes, about two months old, played along the way, wooling one another; falling over and rolling on their backs; tugging at one another's tails, and bothering their patient mother more than they knew while she called them with a low sound; nipped them now and then, and cuffed them to keep them moving.

Never in his life had Trueboy so much

wanted to play. He bounded down the hillside to the mother and little ones.

She whirled and bared her fangs to him.
But big Trueboy was not afraid; he smiled
with his great mouth and wagged his tail so
vigorously, he moved the rear part of his
body. What he was saying was, "I'm just
dying for a romp; I won't hurt anybody."

It was no use.

The wild mother sent the little ones running for cover ahead while she barred the
way, bristling with temper.

Trueboy understood. With head turned
to one side, he sat down, watching the small
mother while she got her young together, and
led them on to the foot of the hill and out of
sight into the tall bushes and grass below.

They disappeared as mysteriously as they
came in sight; Trueboy never saw them again.
It happened, however, that one of the little
ones was less fortunate than the others, for he
was not with the rest of the family that morning and therefore knew nothing of what happened to his mother and the others.

There was a natural reason for this: Young coyotes at this age are very active, so active that sometimes, one larger and stronger than the others fails to mind all his mother's instructions, particularly her warning that they must lie low where she leaves them until she returns. While the mother coyote which Trueboy had seen was away on this morning, little Sharp Nose got restless, wandered away on his own account and mysteriously disappeared.

The wild mother had so many pups that she probably did not miss him when she returned for the others. Possibly she missed him and hunted for him when his trail was too cold to follow. At any rate, she finally was compelled to give him up for lost.

Trueboy held his position watching, while the interesting family passed from sight. Feeling hungry, he sought his hunting ground in the grassy meadow around the lake. He spent an hour here feasting on field mice, ground squirrels and fat insects. His breakfast over, he trotted back to the sunny level space in front of his den, expecting to doze in the warm sun.

Immediately after he lay down a drowsy feeling came over him; he lay with eyes half closed, his head on his front paws, and was almost asleep when he suddenly raised his head.

He saw a small grayish thing moving along a barren trail at the foot of the hill.

Trueboy's eyes were instantly shining, and shining with a light that was expressive of the play-sign. In a few swift bounds he placed himself squarely in front of little Sharp Nose, for it was he, vainly searching for his mother.

Surprised and in utter terror the little coyote tried to run away. This was impossible, for the gigantic Trueboy dropped with his long forelegs around him no matter which way he started. All the while Trueboy wagged his tail and told with his eyes that he was friendly.

Sharp Nose tried to bite but Trueboy paid no heed, only kept up his show of friendliness and finally he licked the small thing, then touched noses with it. After a few more playful moves Trueboy rolled over on his back, inviting Sharp Nose to play.

This was the beginning of a peculiar friendship. Trueboy's gentle nose and his gentle licking tongue, had in some way told the little prairie wolf that all was well here; and once he was convinced, he gave in. He frankly got hold of Trueboy, played only a little at first, then sat back quickly as if he was in doubt still.

Sharp Nose started away, Trueboy following him. Around a sharp turn in the hill was a great rock under which lay a wide space, several feet across. Sharp Nose went in under the rock, Trueboy stood out, looking in and hesitating. It was a big roomy place, with all the front open. He went in.

Sharp Nose did not mind. Trueboy licked him a few times, and in this way reassured him that he felt very friendly toward him.

With this friendship steadily growing, two happy weeks went by. Trueboy led Sharp

Nose to the meadow where he grew fat on bugs, grasshoppers and field mice. Every night they slept together under the rock and every morning they went together to the meadow and swale near the lake.

One morning the order changed. Trueboy and Sharp Nose played as usual when they first came out. Then, remembering he was hungry, Trueboy started off to the hunting ground, but Sharp Nose did not follow. He yawned comfortably and looked after his retreating friend. Perhaps it was because Sharp Nose was more lazy than hungry. Be this as it was, after going down to the little run below and lapping all the water he wanted, he caught a few bugs on the hillside; walked up to the level spot in front of the den and stretched out to sleep in the warm sunlight.

An hour passed with no sound save the drowsy hum of passing insects. Then, far above in the deep blue an eagle soared, a small dot in the azure sky.

Sharp Nose, like any growing puppy, was in a deep sleep.

The dark dot in the sky suddenly grew larger; bigger still it loomed, for the eagle, eyes fixed on the small grayish thing, was dropping swiftly down to the level spot.

At the same moment, Trueboy, having finished his breakfast, was coming back along a bush-bordered rocky trail. The overhanging branches above him sometimes swept his back as he passed under them.

He came into the clearing a dozen yards from the den. At the same instant there was a swoop of giant wings as the eagle sunk his talons into the sleepy puppy. One terrified shriek from little Sharp Nose, and the eagle was in as much terror as his victim. Trueboy rushed; struck swift and sure. He closed on the great bird's thigh; the momentum of the rush rolled him with the eagle over and over to the level below. Trueboy never lost his hold, but shook his victim, the feathers flying in every direction.

SHARP NOSE

Having dispatched the eagle he did not even sniff it, for he was not hungry.

As soon as he was free Sharp Nose rushed under the rock and was too frightened to come out although Trueboy walked up and looked in on him. Trueboy went in; lay down beside the little coyote and licked him gently.

Sharp Nose was never the same after this. A new terror had seized him; he was afraid of everything; somehow he looked at Trueboy in a frightened way.

The next morning Trueboy again went alone to the feeding ground. It was noon before he returned and Sharp Nose was gone; gone completely, for Trueboy hunted around the whole place for him. He never saw him again.

Many things might have happened to the little coyote. It is possible that another eagle was more successful than the first. And there were other enemies—many of them. Yet it is possible that none of these got him. His own wild mother might have come that way and found him.

For several weeks Trueboy smelled for his trail, then gave it up and went back to his solitary habits and existence—an existence that was always troubled, because Trueboy was always lonely and apprehensive. For him it was not a natural life.

Every day and every night he wanted to leave the place, but did not know where to find one better. The wild everywhere was filled with hidden danger and what was worse by far to him than any danger—it was always lonely.

Chapter XVIII

THE NEW DEN

SEPTEMBER came. The days were warm and fine; the cool, sweet nights came down with starlit skies and whispering winds.

As the days of autumn slipped by, Trueboy found it necessary to range wider and wider to find enough food to sustain him. An instinctive knowledge had from the first come to him that the big Timber Wolf and those that followed him did not hunt in this region. Trueboy had never come across their tracks nor discovered the least sign of them from the day he first came to his den above the beautiful little valley. But he remembered that in the old days east of the Big Pine never a week passed that he did not come across their trail.

This was as Trueboy wished, for, although he had grown mighty and powerful, he knew

that the old wolf was deadly. He had no
desire to be brought to a stand by that tremendous enemy alone, much less to be cornered
by him and his followers. It was this instinct
and this wise fear that brought him where
he was, and this same wise fear that kept him
until the frosts came and the game was less
and less. Trueboy did not know, but there
was a reason why no gray wolves hunted in
this locality. As experienced hunters in the
wild, they knew where game might be had,
and, particularly where it might be had when
the deep snows fell, and the north wind came
down in lashing gales that cut to the bone and
killed any living thing which was without
food to warm the blood. Trueboy was alone
in this hunting ground because it was not
good. Except for the little woods around the
lake there was no big timber within many
miles of the place.

October came this year with stinging frosts
and sharp cold north winds that were surpris-
ing so early in the season. With the freezing
of the earth the ground squirrels and all other

small rodents disappeared. At the end of the first week in October a heavy snow fell— a snow that came to stay. With it came bitterly cold days and Trueboy was out day and night. All source of food was swept away as quickly as the cold came down.

One of those strange things in the balance of nature happened with the coming of this unusually early winter.

A plague had struck the rabbits and nearly wiped them out. This foretold the starvation of many lynxes, foxes and, on this fearful winter, even the timber wolves.

It was a winter long to be remembered. The middle of November found Trueboy half starved, but still ranging far and wide in an effort to live in this vicinity. He was so poor his ribs might have been counted. His hair stood up coarse and harsh; his luminous, intelligent eyes shone with an unnatural luster. He fought a constantly losing fight until the last of November, then he came to a decision. Starvation haunted him in this place. He would seek a better one.

One morning he swung away down the canyon while the north wind and spitting sleet cut like a knife. He ran until noon but saw no living thing—only the barren gray rocks and stunted trees. In late afternoon he came out on the open and stood at the edge of the frozen Big Pine River. It was snow-covered in spots; in other places the wind had swept the ice clean. It was a scene such as he had looked upon before; he knew exactly where he was and the danger before him. He stood at full height and looked sharply at the valley on the opposite side. Even in his pitifully emaciated condition, there was that about him as he stood for a time, that would have compelled instant attention and admiration from any human being. Trueboy was a giant dog, half-starved, yet striking in his looks. If ever an intelligent, living being was playing his part in a life-and-death game, Trueboy was playing that part with the last ounce of courage and cunning in him.

He started across the ice; the wind constantly swept the snow in little fine swirls in his face, yet he held to the snow-covered portions and kept his feet while crossing.

It may be that some instinct of nature warned him that if he would enter the enemies' country he should do so on a stormy day when they might not be abroad. Be this as it may, Trueboy at once struck out to seek a den—one much like he had left in the barren grounds in the west.

Trueboy ran up the valley and into the teeth of the wind. He did not stop until he came to a deep-cut ravine where gray bowlders as big as small houses pushed up out of the steep sides and here and there along the bottom.

This place, in view of later events, must be described. Near the head of this ravine, or small gorge, just where the ground began sloping away from the upper level, there was a considerable clump of pine trees. These stood out in marked contrast to the barren snow-covered ground around them. Just beyond this clump of pines, to the south, was the most peculiar rock formation on this vast range. It was known to all cattlemen for miles around as Table Rock. Its name was really a misnomer for it was much like a vast chair that Nature had begun work on centuries before and never finished. The seat of the chair was of solid rock and rose from the ground about five feet. This base or seat was fairly regular in height for perhaps three-fourths the way round on the north, the west and the south. The back of the chair, on the east, was a solid rock formation that shot straight up in the air for at least seventy feet. The top of this shaft was somewhat jagged and tapered at the extreme summit to a width of three feet.

There was nothing more striking than this great Table Rock in this whole country, and it could be seen for many miles from the higher hills.

It was at the head of the ravine near this rock formation and clump of pine trees that Trueboy found what he wanted for a den. His shelter was a hole under a thicket on the north side. This hole was large enough to cover him completely and shield him from the biting wind. He smelled it most carefully when he entered, but no scent came to his nostrils except that of the cold gravel on the bottom and the many little roots from the thicket that in places pushed down through the gravelly soil above.

But the great risk he was taking agitated Trueboy's mind so much that in spite of the seeming safety of the den he came out and hunted up and down the ravine for an hour, trying to find a better hole. His search was in vain, however, and he finally came back to sit outside the hole for a time before he could make up his mind.

At last he went in, but was careful to lay with his head close to the opening so that he could both watch and listen.

Chapter XIX

HUNGER AND DESPERATION

TRUEBOY was content to lie in his shelter until the night fell. Shortly after dark the storm ceased, and two hours later there was not a cloud in the sky.

Trueboy came out, desperately hungry, but luck was with him. He walked up the ravine until he came to a tall lone pine; he stopped there and listened a minute, then walked on until he came under the shadow of Table Rock. He smelled game and it was enticing. But where could it come from? He sniffed and sniffed; incredibly enough it seemed to come from the upper air. A slight sound on the Table Rock attracted him. It was a feathery, flapping sound and with it a snapping, cracking noise. He rushed and leaped, and at one bound stood on Table Rock to rush again at what he saw. A great horned owl barely escaped, leaving nearly the whole of a small rabbit which Trueboy devoured ravenously, leaving not a hair. He did not know that rabbits were now so scarce that he had come upon one almost by a miracle. But perhaps it was well that Trueboy did not know.

He spent some little time smelling over the Rock which the wind had swept bare of snow, but there was nothing more except the freezing, naked stone itself. He leaped lightly down and hunted carefully among the thickset bushes of the ravine. Under a huge rock on the north side he found a long opening but it was not more than six inches high. He smelled food under the rock, reached in with one of his long front legs and raked out a small bone, every bit of which he crunched and swallowed. There was a faint odor of skunk about the place, but if any game lay hidden inside it was impossible for him to reach it.

He hunted down to the end of the ravine

and ran across the level valley several miles
to a long shallow dip in the land which was
covered with heavy pine timber.

He was hunting carefully in these woods
when he trotted out into a little clearing and
square up to a porcupine. Here was food, but
highly dangerous food to those who fell upon
it. Trueboy ran around the bristling, still
thing and once he got too close; with an angry
grunt the porcupine rushed at him. Trueboy
escaped with one of the quills in his nose. He
was wise enough not to try again and when
he had run off a little way and finally got the
quill out of his nose, he started to leave that
part of the timber. He swung on under the
trees and came into a long winding gully
which he followed until it widened into some
timber growing on the foothills. He traveled
for a long distance to the north, keeping in
the woods on the lower level land. Suddenly
he came out into a clearing beside a creek
where there was an old deserted log cabin.
It was a hut left by the wandering trapper,
and his former owner, old Bill Henley. But

long since, Trueboy had forgotten the old man.

He quickly ran back into the woods where he sat down and looked suspiciously at the place. Trueboy remembered his captivity with the Indian trapper and he was not going to take any chance here. After looking at the hut through the trees for some time, something told him it was deserted. He edged in a little nearer, stopped, and with head bent low looked sharply at the place, then ventured the whole distance and put his head in at the half-open door.

There was no scent in the cabin either of man or animal because nothing had been there for a year. There was a fireplace in one end of the hut, and a pile of dry pine boughs lay in one corner. As Trueboy stood inside looking and listening a faint hope struggled in his brain. There was no scent about the hut at all; therefore no sign of an enemy or a friend as yet. But something told the intelligent Trueboy that a human had been here. He was puzzled. Had it been Dan? This

[207]

thought thrilled him with new life. He began vigorously sniffing every part of the dirt floor and even along the side of the log walls, every inch along the fireplace he smelled; then outside of the hut and around in a wide circle he ran, his nose close to the ground as he strove desperately to find the scent that he would follow day and night once he came upon it. But when he had done the only result was his big circular trails with the crust of the snow broken in every direction.

The night was fast coming down. Trueboy came back into the cabin and pawing out a nest among the small pine boughs, he curled up to make the best of it for the night. It was a comfortable bed and Trueboy soon fell sound asleep and dreamed. He seemed to be back in the Valley of the Big Pine running over the green grass and barking back at Dan; and in Trueboy's dream, that seemed so real, he gave little short yelps and his muscles quivered as he seemed to run on ahead of Dan far up the valley; sometimes he ran up hillsides and along winding cattle trails, some-

times over grassy meadows near cool, fresh
streams and always Dan was with him—Dan
who had found him when he was a miserable,
frightened, starving puppy—Dan who had
come to him in that hour and in coming to
him had befriended him and captured his
heart as no other human being could ever
capture it. For hours Trueboy dozed and
dreamed on the pine boughs in the corner of
the hut. Suddenly he awoke, leaping up-
standing on all four feet out in the center of
the cabin. He heard sounds, faint in the distance but still clearly audible.

He went outside and listened. A heavy,
gentle snow had been falling for an hour and
immediately it powdered his jet black coat
with white. But Trueboy scarcely noticed
the snow; with his nose pointed south he listened. There came to his ears the deep wild
roar of the giant wolf and the cries of the
smaller wolves following him. Their howls
sounded steadily nearer as they came on and
it seemed as if they were headed straight toward the timber on the foothills; but just

when Trueboy was getting highly anxious, the sounds swerved to the east and at last they became so faint they could not be heard at all.

Trueboy stood listening for a time to assure himself that his enemies were not coming back, then trotted off to hunt in the near-by woods. He was always hungry and would have remembered his hunger sooner if his thoughts of Dan had not come with such overwhelming force. During the remaining hours of the night he hunted near the cabin, and once went to the summit of a foothill but it was worse there than in the lower timber and he found not even the least odor of a game trail. Even at best the trails of game were few and far between this winter and with a steadily falling snow there was no hope of finding food here. Yet the ever-increasing hunger pangs drove Trueboy on. All night he hunted and the next day; again he toiled through the hours of another night and still another day but he tasted not a bite of food. About the midnight hour of the third night, with incredible toil he dug out a rabbit. This eased his hunger pangs a little. For a week he remained in these woods, dozing at intervals in the hut during the nights, but never sleeping long because of his gnawing hunger. At the end of the week he was desperate. He would seek the heavy timber far to the south of him on the Big Pine River.

With this fixed purpose in mind he set out one early morning in that direction but his hunger was so great he hunted carefully as he went through the unpromising, scattering woods along the base of the low hills. He worked around some thick bushes on a hillside to a level space below covered with a matted growth of brush so thick he could scarcely pass through it, but he plunged on to the edge of this growth where there was a drop of some three feet to a barren place below. As he looked down the hair on his neck stiffened and there shone a wild gleam in his eyes. The tracks of the gray wolves were here and very plain, under the low bush-covered bank and on the snow was the impress of their bodies where they had rested for a time under

the shelter of the bank behind them. The
trail of the wolves led eastward. Trueboy
followed it for a short distance; then threw
up his head and looked. His enemies being
nowhere in sight, he again turned toward the
south and this time he did not pause to hunt
but kept up his rapid pace until he came to his
old den at the head of the ravine near Table
Rock. He went in the hole, and, having satisfied himself that all was well there, came out
and ran for the heavy woods toward the
south; he did not lessen his pace or turn aside
until he was well within the heavy forest.
Then he began his hard search for food.

For four days and as many nights he hunted
in this heavy timber but all he got for his ex-
cessive labor was the bones of a rabbit left by
an owl. On the fifth day he came suddenly
upon a lynx and being desperate, he attacked
the animal, but luckily for him, since it might
have scratched his eyes out, it escaped him
and ran up a tall tree. He did not more than
look for a second up the tree and knowing that
this game was lost he wandered on, hunting

until nearly morning when he came upon a
skunk. In his well-fed days Trueboy would
have spurned this impossible thing but now
in his starving condition he fell upon it, and
devoured the meat as if it had been the choicest of food. The finding of so much meat
greatly encouraged him; he hunted almost
constantly the next two days and nights, but
he got nothing. It was nearly morning of this
second night when he was startled by the cries
of the Old Roarer and the other wolves.
Their wild howls sounded dangerously near
in the dense woods toward the river. Trueboy ran in the other direction, circled widely,
moving out of the woods eastward and on over
the level land, until he came back to his den
near Table Rock. He crawled inside the den
and lay there throughout the rest of the night
and all the next day. Caution warned him to
be extremely careful; he must not again enter
the woods south of him. Therefore, the next
night he came out and stood on the incline
above his den trying to decide which direction
offered the least danger. This night, like

those that were to follow for a continued period, fell clear and bitterly cold. The temperature was thirty below zero. Trueboy stood for a brief time listening but there was not a sound in the clear, still night. He ran down to the bottom of the ravine and sniffed here and there among the bushes until he came out on the level near the tall pine tree. Again he paused, held up his head and listened. He was about to start forward when the sounds that he dreaded floated up to him in the freezing night. The Old Roarer and his followers, now reduced to two, were running up from the south, giving tone to their wild wolf howls as they came. On they came and to Trueboy there seemed but one chance—his den. He ran back down the ravine and into his hole under the bushes; this chance he knew was desperate enough for the entire front was so large that it was open to attack. Trueboy waited, but once more, luck was with him. A scant half mile down the valley the Old Roarer led off to the right, followed a ravine to the upper level and from that point again struck north, his deep roar and the cries of the others passing Trueboy by less than a quarter of a mile on the other side of Table Rock.

All that night Trueboy remained in his den. The next day, until late in the afternoon, he spent hunting among the bushes in the ravine where his den was, then ran down on the valley to search for game trails toward the river. A number of times, as he ran along, he threw up his head and looked longingly at the heavy timber south of him, but when night fell again he ran back to his den. Several times, in the clear, starlit night, he heard the cries of the gray wolves but he did not venture forth for he was afraid to move in any direction. When morning came he started out and hunted much as he had the day before except that he dipped down in the valley somewhat to the east of his den; but he saw no sign of any living thing. As the darkness came he went back to his hiding place, but stayed only a few minutes.

Hunger was gnawing at his life and desperation was upon him. Starving, he was no longer able to feel the caution he had known before. So when the night was an hour old he leaped away to the south woods— the hunting ground where he had found the skunk. He hunted along the upper part of the woods for two critical hours but the very trees, with their silent, low-hanging boughs seemed to be reaching for him with the hand of death. He came out of the woods to make his way upward along a low, wide ravine; when nearly at the head of this his nose struck a scent. He trailed the game to a hole and at the end of two hours, with teeth and fore feet, he dug a rabbit out. He ate it in a few quick gulps and stopped to smell in the hole for more.

Suddenly a lone wolf howl sounded startlingly near, a little to the north. Trueboy ran swiftly to the ridge above and looked over. At the same instant he reached the higher ground, the cry of another wolf came from the east; then sounded the terrible roar of the giant wolf coming down from the northwest and his cry was the howl of a wolf that had struck a trail. The other two wolves sounded the answering call.

Trueboy was miles from his den. It would afford poor enough protection but it was the best he knew. Immediately he thought of it and made a first effort in that direction. He dared not run back down the ravine and out on the valley there, for the giant wolf was coming in from that direction.

Trueboy knew no tricks of the trail. Indeed it may be that he did not even realize that the big wolf had struck his trail. So he did the only thing that the instinct of his brief life told him to, he ran back across the head of the ravine toward the south with the intention of trying to circle the wolf he had heard howl east of him. His reason told him that this wolf was coming to join the other two. This was all he thought or knew. He would run in a wide circle around this wolf to the east and then speed north to his den.

But he miscalculated the position of the lone wolf. In his hurry to run north, Trueboy turned too soon, and, on coming to a rise of ground, ran fairly into the wolf, which was traveling silently westward. There was a short, sharp battle; Trueboy leaped away with all the speed in him for he feared, and feared terribly, to meet all of the enemy. With all his might he raced north but the Old Roarer and the other wolf had heard the sounds of battle and they knew the meaning of the short, wild cries of the pursuing lone wolf. Then Trueboy saw that the thing he had so long dreaded was about to happen. The giant wolf, with continuous roars, swept down the long incline from the west with another wolf close behind. The three came together and rushed Trueboy hard in a narrow valley between two high hills. He strove desperately to increase his lead but the wolves, led several yards by the Old Roarer, kept the pace in a dangerous manner. Luck had at last deserted Trueboy. It was a race to the death and the only hope that came to his tortured mind was that he might reach his den and battle with his enemies there.

Chapter XX

THE FIGHT AT TABLE ROCK

STRAIGHT away over the frozen snow toward the north Trueboy ran. The giant wolf, with the other two at his heels, was dangerously near. In this race Trueboy's enemies had the advantage; no matter which way he turned to dodge them he would be compelled to shorten the distance between him and one of the wolves.

As he ran he looked anxiously from side to side, but there was no way he could turn nearer to his den unless he ran up the steep hill to his left. But the wolves were so close he dreaded to take this chance. A little farther on a thing happened that drove him from his intended course. Before he was aware of it he had run out on the snow covering of a small lake. The snow in places was interrupted and he slipped and floundered dangerously on the ice. The two smaller wolves came on directly behind him; floundered on the ice in the same fashion, and made no gain on him. But the cunning Old Roarer raced around on the solid snow and cut in from the left, so that Trueboy, when he reached the end of the lake, had to plunge hard to the right to escape the monster. This was bad, for Trueboy was thus forced farther out in the valley and he was driven past his den by more than a mile. His instinct told him the truth when he had run too far, and toiling terribly, he whirled to the left with every bit of speed in him, crossed the level land, made the foot of the hill and raced toward the summit. He gained the top; floundered in a treacherous hole; leaped out and again raced away in the clear with the big wolf driving hard upon his heels. Along the summit of the snow-clad hill range Trueboy led them to the south. On this high table land the wily wolves spread out, the two smaller on either wing, the Old Roarer in the center. With their eyes fixed on their prey and the smell in their nostrils they rushed madly to bring him down.

Trueboy ran more than a mile with the howling demons at his heels, and gained not a foot on them.

Suddenly before him, and to his right, loomed the tall pines and the sober, towering shaft of Table Rock, looking solemnly down on the rushing scene.

Trueboy turned sharply to the right and raced straight toward Table Rock. As he came nearer he turned still more to his right, expecting to round the Rock and make his den. But this last turn was almost fatal. The wolf on the right drove in so quickly the big dog was turned back and before he knew it he was up to Table Rock. Not a moment did he hesitate; not a moment did he doubt but gathering himself for the leap as he ran he shot into the air and landed with all four feet upon the rock. All the wolves leaped; the Old Roarer all but made it and clung for an instant with his forefeet but Trueboy whirled and the big wolf dropped to the ground.

The two smaller wolves kept leaping constantly but the giant wolf seemed satisfied for the time. He stood a little off, panting and with head hanging, his deadly green eyes watching the victim, at last brought to a stand.

The other two wolves did not cease in their frantic efforts to gain the ledge, but as often as they leaped Trueboy rushed to the edge and snapped them off.

If Trueboy had been a man he would have seen after a few attempts of these two smaller wolves that they were not capable of leaping up even if unhindered. A number of times each of them had a fair chance when he leaped at the opposite end from that which Trueboy was guarding, but they failed every time they tried it. Their clinging front paws gave way under their noses and they fell back to the snow below. They covered every part of the base of the rock time after time seeking a better way but the stone was precipitous and could not be cleared except by a clear leap.

But unfortunately Trueboy had no way of knowing that these two foes could not reach him. He only knew that Nature prompted him to rush savagely at both wolves every time they leaped for him.

The two smaller wolves worked toward the south end of the ledge where they continued to try to leap up. Trueboy viciously snapped one of them on the nose and charged for the other. Suddenly, behind him, came a mighty roar that carried far in the still night. The big wolf had leaped. Trueboy whirled, and rushed back—but too late. The Old Roarer stood facing him on the Rock.

With instinctive battle sense Trueboy shot back against the solid rock shaft in the rear and with bared fangs faced his enemy. With horrible snarls the big wolf circled. Even his ravenous hunger did not overcome his cunning. He was facing an unusual enemy and he knew it.

With the big wolf on the ledge, the other two lay down below, panting.

Trueboy did not have the experience of his enormous foe but he had a quicker intelligence. In weight they were about equal.

TRUEBOY

Dawn was just breaking. A death-like stillness hovered over Table Rock. A lone star hung dim and pale looking down on the scene. The pines near the Rock stood hushed, silent. The two wolves below suddenly started to their feet, then again dropped down on the snow, panting, watching.

No sound broke the death stillness save the snarls of the Old Roarer and Trueboy as they circled, watching for an opening.

It was soon to be a furious battle.

Chapter XXI

VICTORY

WHILE Trueboy was fighting for his life it happened that Jim Howard and a small number of Joe Hudson's men were at the Ranch on the Big Pine. They had set out from the Brown Bear Ranch following the wide circling Brush Creek where the ground was level and travel was easy, and finally they had swung in from the east to the Ranch house.

There was good reason for their early coming. The reward on the Old Roarer had been increased to six thousand dollars. Joe Hudson had figured up, including the many steers the giant wolf and his small pack had killed in a single night, and he believed the reward was small enough.

And young Dan Hudson—"Dan, every inch a man," as his father always said out of his hearing—decided to make the trip alone.

"You fellows go on, Jim," Dan had said to the foreman, "I can make it in a few days. I'm going straight down the range; in fact I've already got my sleeping places picked out. It may be I'll bring down the Old Roarer while you fellows are getting ready!"

Dan really had no great hope of this so soon and there was a little joking among the men at his remark, Dan joking as much as the others. So, warmly clothed and with enough food to last him, his repeating rifle that he well knew how to use, many rounds of ammunition, and a sharp hatchet, he set out one morning at sunrise.

He made good time the first day, and in the evening came to a canyon where he made his sleeping quarters. He cut a number of pine boughs, part of which he piled back in the hollow of a high bank for a bed. With the other limbs he made a big fire before his sleeping place, and after eating his supper of bread and previously cooked meat he turned in for the night.

About midnight he was awakened by the

cold. He got up, threw more wood on the fire, again covered up in his bed and slept until the dawn was breaking. He stirred up his fire and warmed himself while he ate a hearty breakfast.

As soon as he had done eating he set out again and now began to keep a sharp watch for any signs of the wolves. Much of the time his eyes were on the snow looking for tracks. There might at any time come a chance for a shot and it might all depend on being quick. He traveled all the second day, however, with no sign of the marauders; but there was something about Dan's journey here that he never forgot. He was struck with the fact that he saw fewer signs of living things in the wild than ever before in his life. Only the silent cold and the snow and something like death seemed to pervade all things.

While he made this memorable journey every day fell clear and cold, and every night the moon and stars looked down on his sleeping places, all of which were much like the first.

Over long stretches of level snow Dan traveled on, sometimes dipping down through gorges; at times moving along the summits of low, winding ridges, and again swinging down to the levels of the lower land. But he held fairly steady to a straight course and was well pleased with the good time he was making. He had a naturally long, swinging stride that would have tired many a man, but Dan's sinewy legs seemed never to tire.

As he moved along with only his thoughts for companions he remembered the long lost but never forgotten Trueboy. Mentally he asked himself the question that he had asked so many times, "Why had the big dog left him, and why had he never come back?" And then a small hope came, as it had on that day when all hands decided on the move. The hope was that possibly in the old place, Trueboy would yet turn up; but it had been long since he left and many things could have happened to him. So, after all, Dan's hope was very faint.

He walked on for two hours thinking of Trueboy, the dog that would have been so big and wonderful now if he were still alive. But something, no doubt, had taken him away and he had been held or killed. It must have been so, for Trueboy would have come back if he could.

Dan kept steadily to the south, swinging over miles of level stretches of shining snow; pushing his way through dense willow growths bordering small streams; crossing the ice and angling up long hill slopes to the upper ridges and holding to these until they left the southward trail when he again swung down to the lowlands.

In the early evening of his last night in the open he came in sight of his sleeping place— the deserted log hut of Old Bill Henley. Dan congratulated himself on his progress and was proud of his accomplishment. He knew he could easily reach the ranch on the Big Pine the next day. While he neared the hut through the small trees, the sun dropped out of sight behind the foothills above him on the right. Night would come early here.

As he approached the cabin Dan stopped

suddenly and looked down. Some animal had been traveling around the place, or perhaps more than one, for the snow had been much disturbed. But more snow had fallen since the animal had made the tracks and only the uncertain tracery of the footprints was left.

Dan went on and entered the hut. It was deserted as he expected, but he was instantly interested in the pine boughs in the corner. Some wild animal, he conjectured, had slept there. Possibly the Old Roarer himself. Dan closed the rude door and dropped the wooden peg in place that held the door shut. A strong excited feeling went over him with the thought that the old wolf so much wanted had possibly slept in the hut. Using some of the pine boughs he built a fire in the fireplace and sat down before the comforting warmth to eat his supper. He was tired and shortly after eating turned in for the night in a comfortable place before the fire. He slept soundly all night and awakened before daylight. He got up at once, stirred up the fire and saw by his watch that it still lacked a half hour until daylight, but Dan was like a spirited horse wanting to go. He was so near home now that he believed he could finish the journey by noon.

He started out in the bright moonlight and traveled until daybreak found him on a long open space leading to the south. He was moving toward the clump of pines at Table Rock when he stopped. He heard, as he supposed, wolves fighting there. He listened—yes, he was certain he heard sounds of a desperate battle at Table Rock, just on the other side of the pines.

Dan started at a run across the frozen snow. Again he stopped. He saw two wolves run away from Table Rock toward the north. They had seen him. But they were too far away for a shot. He let them go and ran on. He would get close to the ones battling. The pines would screen his approach.

He reached the thickest pines. The sounds of the battle were tremendous. He stopped and with nervous fingers looked to see that his rifle was working perfectly. He ducked down, pushed quickly in among the pines. There they were up on Table Rock—two giant wolves! He jerked up his rifle to fire, then without knowing what he did, let the gun fall. What were those flashing white feet! Was it—was it—why, yes, as God made him—it was *TRUEBOY!* Trueboy at death grips with the Old Roarer!

The giant wolf drove in twice but like lightning Trueboy met him and fangs clashed fangs. Suddenly the Old Roarer swept in low. There came his savage chop as he reached to crush a front foot. Like a suddenly released spring Trueboy leaped back and saved his foot by an inch. This move of the enemy made Trueboy suddenly realize this danger and he watched constantly to guard against it. Again the giant wolf struck and so swiftly that he ripped Trueboy's shoulder, but the great dog was so quick in his turn that he slashed his enemy twice before he leaped clear. But Trueboy's vicious plunging attack cost him his position. He was now fighting out in the middle of the Rock.

The wolf rushed him constantly and slashed him as often as he rushed. Then Trueboy swept in, his head high. The wolf drove high to meet him. Like a shot Trueboy swept low, chopped for a front foot, missed it and ripped his enemy's foreleg. The wolf slashed for the back but only cut through the skin. Trueboy leaped clear. The wolf came in with such astonishing speed he again ripped Trueboy's shoulder fearfully but Trueboy struck with lightning quickness and tore his enemy's shoulder. In this quick turn Trueboy broke two of his toenails, which he needed almost as much as his fangs.

Then the amazing thing happened in this never-to-be-forgotten battle. Trueboy had been waging a defensive fight but of a sudden the flames of the inborn battler drove him to the attack. With a mighty roar he drove in. Streaming blood from his shoulders, his neck, his flanks, his eyes bloodshot and burning, he fell furiously on his foe.

Ah! that *dog!* No dog could do that with the *Old Roarer*— Yet Trueboy was carrying the attack to him—Trueboy ripped, and streaming blood, but Trueboy, whirling, driving in, pivoting, slashing, chopping, whirling again, once missing his footing, catching himself in a flash, driving in again with terrific rushes. The battle moved like a raging storm over the face of the rock. The quick, horrible snarls of the big wolf, the incessant roar of Trueboy as he drove in with overwhelming, reckless rushes, his hot breath shooting in a cloud of steam—one last terrific drive—Trueboy got the throat—they whirled from the rock, but the great dog held as they fell below, still held—struggled to his feet—and it was over.

"Trueboy! Trueboy!"

The dog looked up; started violently.

Dan was shouting. With a wild cry, half groan, half whine, Trueboy recognized him. In his joy, exhausted as he was, he leaped upon Dan and almost knocked him down. Dan must swear or cry like a baby, so he swore

[234]

with tear-dimmed eyes and he cursed all the wolves in creation; but his swearing meant nothing. It was the only way he could tell his sorrow and his admiration for his starving dog—his dog standing with sharp bones protruding and heaving for breath.

Dan opened his pack and threw out all his food to the dog and while Trueboy gulped it down, whining and crying, Dan put his hands on him, talked to him, petted him and praised him above every dog in the world.

Now the pelt of the giant wolf must be taken and here was more food for Trueboy.

Dan set to work with his hunting knife and as he stripped the skin he cut out portions of the meat and tossed them to the dog.

At last it was done. Dan rolled the great hide, tied it and threw it across his back.

"We'll go home now, Trueboy," said Dan clearing his throat. "Those cuts will heal. Come, Trueboy. We'll go home."

And talking to the dog as he would to a human friend, Dan Hudson started away toward the south.

TRUEBOY

The sun pushed up from the east, flooding the valley with dazzling light. Millions of little particles of frost gleamed and glistened on the vast white sea. And Dan and Trueboy, close together, *very close together,* moved on across the snowy wastes until far down the valley they passed from sight around a bend of trees.